MIKE THE MOOSE,

Master of Marbles

For Children Ages 75 and Under

*To Frank
The President member of
and sole member of
my fan club*

Michael

I Michael Grossman

PUBLISHER INFORMATION

EBook Bakery

www.ebookbakery.com
email: michael@ebookbakery.com

ISBN 978-1-938517-34-1

The actual name of the moose in this book has been changed for no
good reason except that "Francisco the Moose" doesn't sound so good.

DEDICATION

To Susan and Mike the Moose...who is real to us.

To Bijs and Otto Davenport, my grandchildren and Mike's special buddies.

And hoof-bumps from Mike the Moose to some wonderful Grossman related grandchildren: Corazón Grace Adler, Lexie Babbush, Max Babbush, Sam Babbush, Sydney Babbush, Gavin Fitzpatrick, Jonah Fitzpatrick, Maya Grossman, Sadie Grossman, Wyatt Grossman, Morgan Reenders, Mykel Reenders, Sarah Reenders, Alex Rogoff, Grace Rogoff, Joey Rogoff, Emilie Rosen, Olivia Rosen, Ariella Segall, Claire Segall, Elizabeth Segall, Farrah Slonim, and Tobias Slonim.

CHAPTERS

Chapter 1 Mike Finds His Humans.................................... 1

Chapter 2 Mike Discovers Christmas................................. 11

Chapter 3 Mike Goes to Spain 25

Chapter 4 Mike and the Mission 41

Chapter 5 Mike Makes Friends.. 53

Chapter 6 Mike Goes Galactic... 67

Chapter 7 Mike and the Space Ship.................................. 87

ACKNOWLEDGMENTS

Mike the Moose resides with us thanks to the time, attention and caring of some very special Rhode Island based authors, members of the South County Writer's Group. Without them, Mike would still be out wandering in a wilderness of misplaced adjectives and failed thrusts at humor.

Thank you, my dear friends: Agnes Doody (FG), Enid Flaherty, Dave Fogg; Nora Hall, Tracy Hart, Carol Hazlehurst (in memory of), Camilla Lee, Myrina Cardella-Marenghi. Gene McKee, Richard Parker, Jeannie Serpa (a hug), and Virginia Leaper.

A special smile to Carol Hazlehurst, no longer with us, and one of Mike the Moose's favorites except for the times when Mike objected because Carol was funnier than he was. That happened a lot. Bless you, Carol, from all of us.

Mike insisted I give Tracy Hart a special tip of his antlers for her editing and proofreading efforts. It was a hairy job Tracy, and I'm not sure if a tip of the antlers is a good thing or a bad thing. But thank you so much.

Finally, a fist-bump (hoof-bump?) to Susan Mandel, Mike's human mom, for risking her reputation as a sane therapist by cuddling Mike in her lap on frequent airplane trips and showing no concern for the curious looks given by passengers and flight attendants alike.

Hey, if you believe in Mike, he's every bit as real at 40,000 feet.

1
~

MIKE FINDS HIS HUMANS

"Humiliating," thought Mike the Moose. "She crammed me into this cardboard box like a melon." Mike yanked his arm free from a stack of magazines and tugged the strings on his marble sack to get them safely past the end of a pair of rusty garden sheers.

"If that woman sells a thing at this yard sale, it'll be by sheer accident," giggled Mike, delighted by his pun. "What hoofless wonder stuffs a stunningly handsome moose in with a pile of junk?"

Mike snatched the velvet sack free and set the drawstring over his neck. No way would he risk getting separated from the finest collection of marbles in all moosedom, maybe the whole world. It had taken an antler's age to collect them: buying and bartering with other moose at marble meets, on eBay, plus the ones he'd won at marble tournaments. He pulled the pouch open for a peek. All there: his clearie, two cat's eyes, his alley, several toothpastes, an Indian Swirl, a pee wee, a steelie, a milkie, and several more. Mike beamed. His marble collection was the envy of every mooseling. Years of marble study, well maybe four, had paid off in shrewd trades.

Since sunup that morning, neighbors had been stopping by the yard sale to hunt for treasures, although there were few to be had. Several shoppers were less than polite. A boy with sticky hands had yanked Mike out of the box, held him upside down and rudely squeezed his belly before stuffing him back, antler's first. Mike's head narrowly missed the lawn shears as he was squished back next to his pals, Oggie the Purple Orangutan and Gaggle the spotted Giraffe. Like Mike, they bore faded price stickers.

Looking around at broken dishes, splintered furniture and items whose usefulness had long passed, Mike the Moose felt frustrated. "People 'round here don't recognize quality or I'd be on display in a glass cabinet, not this cardboard box. Their lack of sophistication is appalling. What's more, they're unaware of massive intelligence. Humans are hopeless," thought Mike, shaking his antlers back and forth.

Passersby rummaged through a pile at a nearby table. A man with distinctive wire-rimmed glasses, better dressed than most, tried the old Royal typewriter to test the promise on its sticker: WORKING CONDITION. The keys immediately froze in a bunch. A woman in a Hawaiian shirt rummaged through the wicker basket next to Mike, retrieving a tarnished silver spoon which she held to the sunlight.

"How much," she shouted to the lady swatting flies at the cash box.

"Fifty cents apiece," replied the seller. "Real sterling." Her smile revealed yellowed teeth.

The shopper frowned. "Too much. Give 'ya a quarter?"

"Nope," said the seller. "Already marked 'em down once."

"Your loss," said the lady, tossing the spoon back where it bonked Mike on his head.

"Hey, watch it lady," muttered Mike the Moose. "That's moose abuse. Do it again and I'll call the sheriff. I'll demand to see the Justice of the Peace of the Supreme Court. Moose have legal rights too, ya know."

The lady heard nothing; she had moved on to a poster of a parrot at the next table.

A shiny red car angled into an open space in front of the yard.

"Come on, Stephen," said the woman turning to her husband as she exited the front seat. "And you, too, Carrie." She motioned to a little girl in the back seat. "Maybe there's a game CD you don't have."

"I'm fine here, Mom," said the nine year old, eyes peeking from parted strands of blond bangs. Carrie stayed in the backseat and thumbed her iPod.

"You said you would participate. So come on," said Carrie's mom Susan. "Be with us. And brush those bangs back so I can admire you."

"A yard sale. With pushy shoppers?" whined Carrie.

"There's only a few people here," said Susan. "They won't bite."

Reluctantly, Carrie rounded the seatback, one of her earbuds falling out as she did. Her Yankee's baseball cap got mushed, flattening her bangs further over annoyed blue eyes. A braided ponytail swished from the back of her cap as she turned to plead with her mom. "You and Dad can still shop if I stay," said Carrie, fitting the earbud back in.

"Carrie," Susan shot her a look.

"Okay, I'm participating; I'm participating," said Carrie. To make the point she dragged herself to the closest table, feigning interest in a paint-peeled doll house beside the box that held Mike the Moose.

Mike stretched for a better look at Carrie.

Susan, Stephen and Carrie moved along the rows of tables, idly examining the treasures or trash. Stephen fingered a chip on a hand-painted scrimshaw handle, and then eyed a carved, multi-colored walking stick without imperfections. Carrie fist-punched a well-worn catcher's mitt, leafed through a Spiderman comic, and dangled a bracelet of wooden beads, holding them out on her wrist. Susan, a short brunette dressed in slacks and wearing oversized sunglasses, considered a set of historic lighthouse coasters and repeatedly rolled a loose strand of hair back behind her ear. She stopped at Mike's box and looked at Oggie the Orangutan, then finally noticed the brown moose himself.

"Hey Carrie." She held Mike up. "Is he cute or what!"

Mike's antlers rose proudly. "I hope she doesn't see the goo from that kid's hand," Mike worried.

Carrie shrugged.

"It's a miniature moose – a mooseling," said Susan.

"Miniature!" roared Mike the Moose. "You can't be serious."

Susan continued to admire Mike as Carrie shuffled over.

"There is nothing little about me, Madam. I am Mike the Moose, Master of Marbles, and don't you ever understate my prodigious proportions, especially my antlers which grow every day. "What is little, Madam, is your intellect if you can't appreciate how big they are!" Mike said in an enormous huff. "Nobody likes to be patronized, especially we moose."

Mike's complaints went unheard of course.

"Have a look, Carrie," said Susan holding Mike up.

Acting disinterested, Carrie looked first at several other items, picking up a worn bat and swinging it before she reached her mom.

"A moose, yeah," she grunted, shrugging. "How much longer Mom?"

Susan put Mike back in the box. "I'm ready when you and Dad are," she said.

"Thank goodness," thought Mike the Moose, swallowing disappointment, "who'd want to live with them? The mom was okay. But that little girl…what a Grinch. It'd probably unravel her braid if she smiled."

"Still," thought Mike as his antlers sagged just a bit, "I'd sure like a family."

He proudly pushed himself up from the rusty sheers.

"Carrie," Stephen called, "you ready?"

"Yup," said Carrie, returning a jump rope to its box.

Carrie neared Mike's box, but stopped, hoping her mom wouldn't see her check out Mike again.

"What's she doing?" wondered Mike. "This girl isn't clever enough to appreciate my magnificence." But his heart beat considerably faster. Carrie lifted Mike up. The hint of a smile tugged the corners of her cheeks as she ran her finger over Mike's beakish nose. Mike tried to act nonchalant, but his Moose eyes grew wider and he couldn't hold back a toothy grin. Carrie turned him over.

"Kid, I'm no melon," protested Mike. But catching himself, he softened his prickliness and gave Carrie a wink which she missed.

Susan approached and took Mike from Carrie.

"Adorable," she said and handed him back. "Cute, huh, Carrie?"

Carrie's interest seemed to fade again and she stuffed Mike the Moose back in the box and walked away. But a moment later she turned back once more, this time with a full smile when she reached Mike.

"Let me treat you to him, Carrie," said Susan. "My gift."

"Nah," said Carrie, but she didn't turn away.

"You rarely ask for much. Let's bring him home," said Susan, lifting Mike from the box. She carried Mike to the cash box lady.

Mike practically swooned. "*Home.* She did say home." He shouted back to his friends in the box, "Hey, Oggie. Gaggle. I think I'm getting a home. With a family. I promise to put in a good word for you guys when the time is right. I'll really miss you guys," said Mike waving goodbye. "See you soon I hope."

Mike's grin fell. Oggie and Gaggle were his best friends.

The lady at the cash box wiped her dripping brow. "Take a buck for it," she grunted.

"'It. A dollar. A single dollar," said Mike outraged. "Why you old porcupine, I'm worth $50 if I'm worth a penny. I demand a markup!

"$46.50?" Mike negotiated but no one heard him.

Susan handed her a dollar and the woman reached for a wrinkled paper bag.

"No need for the bag," said Susan. "Save the trees, you know," she said, smiling.

The woman looked blank.

"So my new mom's green-conscious. That's good to find in a mom who's non-moose," thought Mike. "She's clever too – stopping that wretched lady from stuffing me in a paper bag. Why I could suffocate or have a bad dream."

As the car exited the yard, Susan handed Mike the Moose to Carrie in the back seat.

"He's terribly cute, Carrie," said her mom. "You should name him."

With uncharacteristic interest, Carrie lifted Mike until they were face to face, pretending her new gift could talk.

"Any ideas what I should call you, Mr. Moose? We can't have a family member with no name."

"*Family.*" The word swelled through his fur like music. "Family. My family." It sounded even better then he'd dared imagine.

The moment he knew he'd at last found his family, Mike's antlers trembled. It had never happened before. His eyes fluttered and his hoofs twitched as if an electric spark had passed through and sent tingles along every strand of his fur. His legs, feeling like noodles, gave way, and Mike dropped in a swoon, dizzy, his vision blurry. Everything went dark – dark as the deepest forest at midnight.

Moments passed before Mike's vision cleared and his world rippled back.

"What just happened?" he wondered, rubbing his eyes. "Was it lightning? Did a cloud pass over the sun?"

"Suppose I call you Penelope. Penelope Moose," Carrie said, mimicking the English accent of a nanny she'd seen on TV.

"But he's a boy moose," said Susan. "Boys have antlers. I don't think you should call him Penelope."

"PENELOPE? Are you kidding?" Mike the Moose turned to Carrie. "Maybe I should call you Carrie Canoodle?" said Mike. "Of course I'm a boy moose, for goodness sake. And, Missy Carrie Canoodle, do you honestly think a moose of my fame has no name? I suppose some stork dropped me from a cloud – nameless?"

Stephen slammed on the brakes and brought the car to a tire-smoking stop. Susan froze. Carrie dropped Mike and dove for him as he hit the floor.

"Oppffff," groaned Mike as Carrie's catch choked his tummy.

"Sorry," said Carrie, loosening her grip, though she felt pretty stupid talking to a toy.

"Humans need so much help," muttered Mike, straightening his antlers.

Susan, trying to get words out, looked like a goldfish out of water.

"Tell me you heard it too, Susan?" Stephen said.

"I swear it spoke!" said Susan, her eyes fluttering.

"IT? I'm an 'IT' again," huffed Mike the Moose.

All three of them turned to him.

"That thing…moose…it talked," said Stephen.

"No way," said Carrie, looking confused, her blue hat askew.

"I heard it," said Stephen.

"Duh," said Mike the Moose. "Of course I speak. I am practically three…which in people years is…ah…7 times 3 divided by 3 plus 1…is nearly 8," said Mike calculating on his hooves. "Although I admit for 8 I'm unusually articulate."

The three just stared. Mike decided they all needed a tan.

Susan finally formed her sentence. "You spoke words!"

"Duh," said Mike growing impatient. "Of course I use words. You expect sign language maybe? Dancing with hooves? Antler signals? A 'Yo' sent telepathically?"

"But," Susan said, "but you're just a…"

In a flash of mom instinct, Susan restrained herself from saying…"toy." That was a good thing, because calling Mike a "toy" was never a cool move.

"But you're just a…a small moose," Susan rephrased.

"Madam…Mom…and all of you in my new family. If I'm coming home with you, you need to get clear on a few things," insisted Mike.

"FIRST. Like I said. I'm a boy moose, surely no girl.

"SECONDLY. My full and proper moose-given name is Mike the Moose, and my title is Master of Marbles," said Mike, motioning to his velvet sack. "You will find I'm quite an expert on that subject as anyone who is up with the world of marbles knows."

"THIRDLY. I am exceptionally bright. I know that's obvious, but Gaggle the giraffe says I'm pre…pre…pre …precocious." The word came out like a sneeze.

"FOURTHLY. I have these grand, handsome antlers…that's obvious, but they do need to go sideways through certain doors.

"FIFTHLY. I expect to sleep in the same room with my new sister, Carrie. I don't like to sleep all alone.

"And SIXTHLY. I am really afraid of crockigators – there aren't any at home are there?" asked Mike, clearly concerned.

After a stunned pause, Carrie spoke first.

"Nope, Mike; we don't have a single crocodile or alligator. Or crockigator. Though I have other stuffed…"

Carrie stopped mid-sentence, realizing like her mom that she was about to blow it. "…that is…I have other small animal creatures like you. Dolls."

Mike scowled.

"Not that you're a doll, Mike. Just cute like one. You're real of course. But I do have Boris the bat, Buffie the buffalo, Mousey the mouse, and Honks the duck. Oh and Pogo my purple piglet."

"I do like friends," considered Mike the Moose. "In fact, I'd really like to meet them…" Mike paused a moment before continuing…"as long as they know I'm their BIG brother," said Mike raising his antlers.

"They stay in my bedroom, too," said Carrie, trying to be firm.

Mike tapped his front hoof.

"But, ah," said Carrie, "they sleep in my Radio Flyer wagon."

"Which is not where I sleep, of course," said Mike.

"Oh no," said Carrie. "You're in my bed?"

Mike nodded approvingly.

The car arrived at a brown-shingled house. A flower-lined walkway led to a red door with a big brass mail slot.

"Welcome home," said Susan warmly.

Mike grinned.

"This is the living room Mike," said Carrie as if starting a tour. They entered a large room with a stone fireplace in the corner.

Mike heard the pounding of a hundred hooves, or so it seemed, then growling and barking.

"Bolt the doors!" Mike screamed. "It's crockigators, OMG."

Mike's antlers rose in full alarm.

But the door had no bolt and the home had no crockigators, although three large dogs bounded into the living room, panting, circling, barking and wagging.

"Mike," said Stephen. "Carrie forgot to mention our dogs. Meet Kola, Cooper and Eddy. They're family too."

"Yeah," said Carrie, "we have dogs."

"Dogs," repeated Mike the Moose, "…flea-laden creatures that scratch and want walks? Seriously? Dogs?"

Cooper, Kola and Eddy were curious. Carrie held Mike the Moose away from them but Cooper managed to nuzzle his snout into Mike's belly. Mike nearly fainted.

"No, Cooper," said Carrie. "Down, buddy."

Cooper wagged then sat.

"Okay, Cooper, get a bone," said Carrie.

Cooper trotted off while Carrie tried to comfort Mike the Moose who lay prone in her arms, mumbling something she couldn't follow.

"Dogs? I like my new house…and my humans. But dogs? That's a bit much," thought Mike the Moose, shaking his antlers.

That afternoon Susan and Stephen came to Carrie's bedroom.

"We need to go out," said Susan. "Will you two be happy playing in your room? You can watch TV or play a game?"

"I'm tired of the games I have," Carrie objected.

"Carrie…" Susan said.

"Okay, okay," said Carrie hopping on the bed with her sneakers on.

"Shoes, please," said Susan.

Carrie kicked off her Nikes. "Mike. Could I see your marbles?"

Mike the Moose considered. He'd imagined he'd be going everywhere with his folks when they went out. On the other hand, his antlers felt droopy.

"Okay, I could use some down time," Mike said to Carrie.

Mike opened his pouch and allowed a few of his marbles to roll out.

"Gosh Mike," said Carrie picking up a large cleary, "this one's beautiful."

"Yeah, and this one too," said Mike showing her his prized Tiger's Eye. "This one's an antique and very valuable."

Carrie held it to the window light.

"Do you know that marbles go way back," explained Mike, "to ancient Egypt. I wasn't born yet. There are marbles mentioned in Roman writings too. But those marbles were stone. The glass one's came in 1903. When this guy in Ohio invented a machine just to make marbles," said Mike.

"You sound like my home-room teacher," said Carrie.

She picked Mike up, cradled him in her arms and set him gently on top of a big fluffy white pillow. In no time at all, Mike's eyes began to close and he felt Carrie's cheek on his own.

"Welcome home Mike the Moose," Carrie said. "Welcome, little moose brother."

"Thanks, Carrie," said Mike the Moose. He liked the sound of his new sister's voice. He loved calling Susan "Mom" and Stephen "Dad."

"Hey Carrie?" asked Mike, lifting up on his hooves.

"What Mikey?" Carrie turned.

"This is my full-time home right? You guys don't do yard sales?" he asked trying to sound casual.

"Mike," said Carrie, "this is your forever-and-ever home and you are as much a part of this family as I am."

A huge smile spread across Mike's face. It had been a totally acceptable morning.

2

MIKE DISCOVERS CHRISTMAS

Stephen's eyes blinked open in stages. The first up, as usual, he slipped quietly from bed so as not to wake Susan and did a reach-for-the-ceiling stretch. Cooper, the collie, heard him stir and arrived for his master's good-morning head pat. Kola, a husky mix and not a morning dog, was in a grizzly mood. (Honestly, Kola was rarely in a good mood even midday or at night.) Kola growled at Cooper for making noise, seeing no reason why dogs or humans should be interrupted from a good night's sleep. The last of the pack, Eddy, a black Lab mix, arrived next, his tail rotating like a helicopter propeller.

In the next bedroom, Mike the Moose (on the pillow next to Carrie), awoke too, stirred by tree branches scratching the window pane in the strong wind. From where he lay Mike could see leaves swirling outside and tree limbs bending like fishing poles.

"Morning, Mike the Moose," said Carrie, stirring.

She headed for the bathroom to brush her teeth, wondering how Mike kept his so white when she hadn't seen him with a toothbrush. Upon her return, Mike, teeth gleaming, smiled. "Time for breakfast?"

"Yep, let's head done," Carrie said, and the two headed downstairs.

The coffee brewed, the toaster popped, and Susan placed slices of golden brown cinnamon-raisin bread on a large yellow platter. In the corner Eddy, Kola and Cooper munched, crunched and slurped heaping bowls of dog meal.

Mike noticed that Susan had almost finished setting up her Christmas Village on the curio shelves along the walls in the living room. Trains on tracks circled a miniature village past ceramic churches, homes, banks, and a red brick post office. Cotton snow looked almost like the real thing. There were mechanical Christmas elves and a rocking reindeer that, if you pushed his button, swayed to the tune of *Jingle Bell Rock*. Skaters twirled around a mechanical rink, and a battery operated Santa twisted to *Rudolph the Red Nosed Reindeer*.

"My new Mom is into Christmas big time," thought Mike. "Holidays will sure be fun."

Susan picked up Mike and held him to her face.

"The one person I haven't shopped for is you, Mr. Mooseling," she said with a wink. "What should I tell Santa our newest family member wants?"

"Wow," thought Mike. "I never got a Christmas present before."

In fact Mike had never considered the possibility of getting a Christmas gift.

After a moment's pause he said, "Well, is there any chance, could I have, I mean if it's not too much, ah, you see I have this collection." Mike proudly opened the bulging velvet sack he carried.

"What's that Mike?" Susan said.

"My marble collection. Probably the finest ever. I've traded for some of them with Oggie and Gaggle, collecting practically forever…since I was this little," said Mike raising his hoof to mouse height. "I have all different kinds from lots of places. I have star marbles, several clearies, some biggies and smallies. You have to admit Mom, it's just about the most beautiful marble collection ever. See…," said Mike, taking marbles out one at a time.

"They are beautiful, Mike," Susan said. "Blue, pink, and even a gold one...and I love this clear one. Ooh, here's one with a star that sparkles inside. What a brilliant collection!"

"I have twenty-four Mom," he said, his chest stretching out.

"So you would like more for Christmas?" Susan asked.

"Well, one more would make twenty-five...a perfect number. Twenty-five is one fourth of a hundred, you know," Mike said, demonstrating mathematical sophistication.

"I could put in a word with Santa," Susan said. "He's pretty good at knowing what kids want...what mooselings want too, I bet." She winked at Stephen, who grinned as he reached for more toast.

After the breakfast dishes were put away and Susan, a high school Spanish teacher, had finished grading papers, she announced she was leaving for the mall. Although she usually preferred to stay at home, Carrie surprised her by asking to go.

"Wonderful, Carrie," said Susan. "You hardly ever want to go Miss Shy One. It'll be great to have your company."

"Let's go, Mike," said Carrie, sweeping Mike the Moose into her backpack. Mike's head perched above the flap. "We're off to the mall, Mr. Moose."

"Neat," said Mike. "What's a mall?"

"It's stores but really big," said Carrie. "Store after store and you can buy just about anything."

"It's not like a yard sale, is it?" asked Mike, looking anxious.

"No way, Mike," Susan interrupted overhearing Mike. "We're shopping for presents ...maybe even for a Christmas marble."

"Oh," said Mike, looking relieved and then excited.

"But one other thing, Carrie," said Mike.

"Yeah?"

"This mall. It's not a place with crockigaters, is it? I'd just as soon not go if it has them. I don't like crockigators...especially their crooked teeth."

"Not to worry," Carrie said. "None of those...and you'll be with me."

"Or kids with gooey hands? Kids pull my antlers and get me sticky."

"There are lots of kids at malls, Mike. Crowds, too, but I won't let them touch you. You'll be fine with us," said Carrie doing a hop to center her backpack. "Besides we need your help to shop."

"'Okay,'" said Mike the Moose smiling.

Mike had never seen anything like the mall. It was way bigger than a yard sale. They passed a bazillion stores with colorful signs and window displays and mannequins that looked alive but didn't move. And a gazillion kids with drippy spoons of frozen yogurt, tied to iPods through earbuds. They eyed Mike but if they approached, Carrie swung her backpack to the front to keep Mike safe from their sticky grasp.

"Is there a Marbles-R-Us?" asked Mike as they passed Toys-R-Us.

"No stores just for marbles," said Carrie, "but Grimbles has a huge toy department with marbles in lots of sizes and colors."

"You can choose any marble you want," said Susan. "I'll tell Santa."

"Any one?" said Mike.

"Yep," said Susan.

"But don't they cost a lot?" asked Mike. "I had to trade my wood slingshot for one clearie."

"Any. One. You. Want," said Susan.

Mike glowed.

Susan saw a sweater she liked for Carrie.

"Try it on," Susan urged.

It was wool and pink with a Christmas elf holding a kitten.

"I have enough sweaters, Mom."

"Try it on, Carrie," Susan urged.

Carrie set her backpack down. She slipped the sweater on and stood back to see herself in the mirror. Neither of them noticed the greasy hand that reached around the sweater table. It wrenched Carrie's backpack off the table and hurried away while Carrie modeled for her mom.

"Let me see you from the side," said Susan. Carrie turned to a different angle.

Mike the Moose didn't know what happened. He felt a terrible tug that knocked him to the bottom of Carrie's backpack. Next thing he knew he was bouncing in darkness, antlers knocking into Carrie's hair brush. The rough ride didn't feel right. Carrie always carried him carefully. Yet there he was in the dark, rear up, antlers down at the bottom of the backpack, swung wildly in all directions. Mike felt as if he was on the Tilt-A-Whirl at the amusement park. He tried repeatedly to right himself but was thrown back each time.

"Carrie, I'm seasick," he yelled.

But Mike was bounced as roughly as ever. Gathering strength he made a determined effort to sit up and this time succeeded in popping his head above the rim of the backpack. His little moose jaw dropped wide open. Carrie wasn't carrying him at all. It was a kid, a greasy-haired teenager who Mike guessed was really old…maybe fifteen. He had streaked hair and a cap worn to the side, freckles, a ring in an ear, and a chain on his chest. Mike's eyes bulged when he saw the kid's scary black T-shirt. On the back was a picture of a guitar, but the base curved into a bleeding, red skull, and below the skull were faded orange words: *Death Buzzard Band.* The kid speed-walked just short of running, glancing back every few seconds.

"Help, Police, Emergency," screamed Mike. No one heard him. "911, 411, amber alert, code blue, SOS, Mayday?" Mike yelled as loud as he could.

No one looked up.

"Are you nuts?" Mike screamed at the teenager. "Take me back to my sister this instant," he demanded.

The kid kept speed-walking.

Meanwhile, Carrie decided she didn't like the pink sweater, returned it to the table and turned for her backpack.

"Huh, I thought it was right here. Must have left it over there," she thought, walking to an adjacent table. It wasn't there either.

"Mom do you have my backpack?" asked Carrie.

"Didn't you leave it on the sweater table?" said Susan.

"I set it right here," said Carrie, tapping the table.

"Oh no," thought Carrie. "It has my house keys and my brush and…" Suddenly Carrie's face got an awful look.

"And MIKE THE MOOSE," she said. "Mom. Mike the Moose!"

Carrie and Susan searched the area frantically – no backpack. Susan hurried to a checkout counter.

"Call security immediately, please," Susan said. A bored looking salesclerk slowly looked up, lazily pushing her eyeglasses further up her nose. She stared blankly at Susan.

"CALL SECURITY," said Susan. "PLEASE. NOW. There is a thief in the mall and my daughter's backpack is gone."

Slowly, mechanically, the salesclerk reached for a button under her register and waited, chewing her gum until a man in a blue security uniform appeared.

"What's up, Marge?" he said.

"Someone took my daughter's backpack," Susan answered for the clerk. "While I was trying on sweaters at that table," Carrie pointed.

"You sure it's gone?" asked the guard.

"Totally sure, Sir," said Susan. "We looked all around several times."

"Show me where," said the guard. He said something into the walkie-talkie clipped to his shoulder as they walked to the table. A second security guard holding a clipboard arrived.

"Handbag's contents?" he asked Carrie, writing as she answered.

"Cell phone, wallet, about $10 cash…hairbrush," said Carrie. Oh… and one of my mom's credit cards." Carrie was reluctant to mention Mike, fearing the guard wouldn't understand.

"That's right, my MasterCard, Carrie," said Susan. "I forgot I'd given it to you."

"But Sir, another thing…" said Carrie.

"Yes?" The guard looked up.

"Our moose…I mean mooseling. Mike the Moose!" Susan interrupted urgently.

"Your what, lady?" asked the guard staring at Susan. "I mean Ma'am."

"Our mooseling. A little brown moose with tall antlers!" said Susan.

The second guard looked at the first guard.

"Say what?"

"He's really important," Susan said. "He was in my daughter's backpack. We just got him a few days ago. He's part of our family. We have to get him back."

The officers exchanged "going-to-be-one-of-those-days" looks.

"Oh sure, lady. A moose."

Susan glared at the officer.

"He means we'll do our best, Ma'am," said the second guard.

The first guard said something into his walkie-talkie and left.

The greasy-haired teenager climbed into a car with Carrie's backpack under his arm like a football. Peeking over the flap, Mike saw he had two friends waiting, and quickly ducked down.

"How much we get?" said the driver who appeared slightly older than the other kids.

"Didn't have time to check," muttered the surly teenager. He started to rummage through Carrie's backpack.

"Give me that," said the driver, snatching it away.

"Set of keys…here we go, a wallet." He thumbed through the contents. "Ten lousy bucks. Let me guess. You took a kid's backpack, bonehead," growled the driver.

"Wait, here we go," said the thief, taking the backpack back. "A credit card. Still valid too."

"At least you got something," complained the driver.

"What's that?" said the quiet kid, peering through his glasses at something that had fallen on the car floor. He picked up Mike.

"Unhand me. Let go. Crime never pays," hollered Mike the Moose.

"Just a stupid stuffed toy," said the driver, tossing Mike back on the floor. "Which confirms that the backpack you took belonged to a kid, you whack job," said the driver.

"What an idiot," added the third thief.

"Hey? We got a credit card out of it – not just a stupid stuffed toy," said the pimply teenager. "And hey, I did all the work. You guys just sat here."

"How dare you call me a toy…or stupid…or stuffed," Mike the Moose bellowed from the floor.

The thieves studied the credit card.

"You guys deaf as posts? Call me stupid. You're heading for big trouble…a jail cell maybe…so you aren't so smart. While I'm a member of Moose MENSA with the highest IQ on record. Well, one of the highest. And you call me 'stuffed?' Judging from this pig pen of a car," Mike pointed his hoof to dozens of crumpled, yellow Super-Pounder with Cheese wrappers scattered on the floor, "if anyone is stuffed, it's you three. Don't you know you should eat organic? We moose do."

Mike stood tall, his antlers fully erect, confronting abductors who couldn't hear him.

The driver held up the card.

"How can we use it? None of us looks like a "Susan," he said pointing to the name on the card.

"Call Melissa. Get her to buy stuff," said the backpack stealer.

"Hold off a minute," said the quiet one. The Red Sox cap he wore backwards was way too big and practically covered his glasses. "Ripping off a backpack is one thing; credit card theft is a whole 'nother ball game."

"Big deal. Melissa uses it this afternoon, then we trash it," said the driver.

As they argued, Mike saw his chance. He squeezed under the front seat, inching forward towards keys that hang off the steering column. He had to slide past the driver's unlaced tennis shoes which smelled like Sammy Skunk when he got scared and sprayed. Mike felt dizzy, but he inched bravely onward until finally, standing on his two back hooves, he could just about reach the car keys – but not quite. His stretched hoof fell an inch short.

"Maybe I can fork them with my antler," thought Mike, stretching harder.

"Who made you boss?" the greasy-haired teen shouted, grabbing the credit card from the driver.

While the three quarreled, Mike slid his antler into the key ring. An enormous antler shake loosened them and they dropped to the floor. Hip hop from the radio muffled their fall.

Mike squeezed back under the front seat. Halfway to the back seat, he hooked the keys on a broken seat spring as the three teens reached a decision about the credit card.

"Dude," said the quiet kid to the driver, "we need to beat it."

"I have to get out of this car," Mike thought.

"Yeah," said the driver. "Let's roll." He patted the ignition switch. "Who's got the keys?" he said.

"I don't have 'em," said the kid with glasses."

"You had them," said the surly thief.

"Very funny. This is no time to mess around. Gimme them. Now," said the driver, shaking a fist.

"I don't have 'em."

"Me neither," shrugged the other kid.

The driver searched his jacket a third time and looked worried.

"Come on, get off your butts and start looking," he said, exiting the car.

"Butts not a nice word," said Mike from the back seat. "Carrie told me to use 'rear.'"

The three searched around the parking space.

"I know what else I can do!"

He inched again to the driver's seat. Standing behind the wheel on his hind hoofs, reaching as tall as he could, he pushed on the horn with all his might: one, two, three times. The old car's horn beeped twice but on the third honk the horn stuck and blared on without stopping.

Mike scrambled back beneath the front seat and into Carrie's backpack.

"What's with you, dingbats? Who hit the horn?" yelled the driver. He banged repeatedly on the horn. "Won't stop."

Mike had to hold a hoof over his mouth he was laughing so hard, not that his abductors could hear him anyway.

The three thieves lifted the hood and frantically searched for the horn wires, cupping their ears while they did.

The greasy-haired teenager was first to realize how much trouble they were in when he saw the white and black mall security car, red light flashing, heading towards them.

"Dump the backpack NOW," he yelled, tossing it to the driver.

The driver caught the backpack and ran. Once again Mike felt like a shirt in a clothes dryer. The driver ran to a trash can and quickly stuffed the backpack deep in the garbage. Then he walked nonchalantly back to the car as if he was whistling, which he wasn't.

The squad car pulled up next to the honking car and one of two security guards rolled down his window. "Problem boys?"

"Nope," said the driver. "Stuck horn."

"Turn the key on and off," suggested the guard. "That can clear a stuck horn."

The three teenagers sat motionless.

"It's worth a try kid," urged the guard.

"We don't have the keys," said the driver.

"We…we lost 'em," said the backpack thief.

That reply interested the guards and one of them got out of the squad car.

"Why don't you show me your license and car registration, boys.

His partner called the local police station with the license plate number.

"How'd you manage to lose your keys?" the guard asked. "Where were you in the mall? At what stores?"

"The key was in the ignition," said the quiet kid with glasses.

"We haven't been in the mall yet," lied the surly teenager.

"Yeah. We haven't been to the mall yet," said the driver.

The guard, a beefy man, noticed a half-eaten ice cream cone melting on the pavement. It was his favorite–a Double Dipper Death by Chocolate cone and you could only get them at the mall.

"Did you check under the seats?" said the guard.

"We did, but they're no keys there," muttered the driver.

From inside the trash can, Mike the Moose struggled to see over the top of the backpack. Something didn't feel right. Maybe it was the half-eaten peanut butter and jelly sandwich stuck unceremoniously to the top of his head. He peered up slowly over the flap looking like a poor moose imitation of Napoleon Bonaparte.

"There has to be a way to catch the guard's attention," thought Mike. "If I tip this trash can over maybe he'll hear the racket and come to check it out."

Mike rocked, back and forth, but the can hardly budged. He tried harder. No results.

In the distance Mike saw a weather-beaten dog sniffing from can to can, zigzagging closer. Mike put two hooves to his mouth and produced his best baseball stadium whistle. The old dog's ears perked up and his tail wagged excitedly as he headed to the trash can. He sat at the base of the can, wagging and looking up at Mike.

"So," Mike said to the mutt, "I bet you can't do what dog's do at trash cans."

The scruffy dog rose to Mike's challenge. He shook to unwrinkle his fur, then balancing on three legs, raised the fourth slowly and leaned into the can. The can tipped from the dog's weight, and as it did, Mike ran at the can's side. His timing was perfect. The can teetered and finally... boom! It thundered down, spilling papers, old shopping receipts, a banana peel and a sun-bleached copy of *Teens Today* magazine onto the pavement. Carrie's backpack dropped out too. But Mike? He was stuck in the can, half visible, half buried in trash. The mutt ran off, frightened by the crash.

Startled by the noise, the guards looked up. The burly one strode to the trash can while the three teens looked on nervously, fighting the instinct to run.

"What's this?" said the guard, spotting the backpack.

"Finally," muttered Mike the Moose from the trash bin. "What took you so long? I, Mike the Moose, am not accustomed to my spending afternoons in a trash can."

The officer picked up Carrie's backpack and turned away, leaving Mike in the can, unseen, the half-eaten sandwich still on his head. Mike's antlers sank.

The big guard stopped. Something he'd seen had just registered and he turned back. He pushed aside a faded newspaper. There was Mike the Moose who looked about as disheveled as a proud mooseling ever does.

"It's about time," huffed Mike. "When I shop at a fancy mall, I expect quality protection! What's the point of rescuing Carrie's backpack if you leave me in this trash? I have your badge number. It's a good thing you came back."

The guard heard nothing but cocked his head into his lapel radio.

"Hey Ed, it's Jason. Didn't the lady mention a stuffed toy?" he asked into his walkie-talkie.

"Stuffed?" hollered Mike. "From you who look like the Michelin Tire Man. And how dare you refer to my distinguished personage as a "TOY!" said Mike wiping peanut butter off an antler.

The hefty guard dangled Mike upside down by a hoof.

"Yeah, it could be a cow. Maybe a buffalo?" said the officer.

Mike snorted and shook the air with his antlers. "Buffalo! What Police Academy graduated you, Sherlock? Do a moose and a buffalo have even one thing in common?" said Mike, his fur turning an unnatural shade of red.

"A moose? Yeah…might be a moose," the guard confirmed holding Mike higher. "Tell the kid to calm down. We have her doll."

"Doll!" groaned Mike the Moose. "Officer, you just won an all-expenses paid trip to an ophthalmologist. This is over the top."

"I'll bring it to her. Have the lady meet us at security," said the guard heading for his squad car – Carrie's backpack in one hand and Mike, upside down, in the other.

The town police arrived and the three thieves sat in the back seat of their squad car behind a steel divider.

"I warned them, crime doesn't pay!" said Mike, waving a hoof. "Now who looks dumb?"

Susan and Carrie had run to the mall's security office, arriving out of breath.

"Oh, Mikey," said Carrie lifting him from the guard's hand and wiping the last traces of peanut butter off his antler. "I was so worried, and I'm so, so glad you're back. What a terrible first visit to the mall. Thank you so much, Officer Sir." Carrie smiled shyly.

"Yes, thank you, Sir." Susan shook the guard's hand vigorously like it was a pump.

"No problem, Ma'am. I think you'll be wanting these too?" he said, handing Carrie's things back. "Your cell phone, the backpack, a wallet, and your credit card."

Carrie held Mike so tight he felt the circulation fail in the last two inches of his antlers.

"Carrie, you're suffocating me," gasped Mike, squished against his sister's chest.

Carrie didn't care; she was so happy to have him back. She couldn't let go.

"I'll never lose you again, my little mooseling brother," she vowed.

"Where to next, Mom?" asked Mike as the car turned from the mall parking lot.

"Home," Susan said. "We're taking you home."

On the ride home, it occurred to Mike that he never got to shop for his marble. Carrie read Mike's mind and smiled. Susan had whispered that she'd go back to buy one before Christmas.

A few days later, unbeknown to Mike, she did, returning home with not one but three amazing additions for Mike' collection: a small peppermint swirl, a purie, and the largest – a cat's eyes, red with black squiggly lines.

They were great treasures but not as important to Mike as the family he got for Christmas. That was the big reason Christmas turned out to be Mike the Moose's best one ever; not to mention his first.

3

MIKE GOES TO SPAIN

"Did the tickets come?" Susan asked Stephen who was thumbing through the mail.

"From NorthStar Travel?" Stephen asked, handing her a thick, white envelope.

"Great," she said, removing two airline tickets.

"There's a mistake," said Mike the Moose, looking up from Carrie's lap. "Two tickets? Doesn't Carrie get to come too?"

"Not to worry, Mikey," Carrie said. "Mooselings travel without a ticket. In my backpack."

"I'm not so fond of your backpack, Carrie," said Mike.

"It won't happen again," Carrie said, clutching Mike tightly.

"Maybe it won't..." said Mike with little conviction.

"I won't let you out of my sight. You can ride in my lap on the plane."

"I wish Dad could come," Carrie said.

"So do I, honey," said Susan. "But he has too much piled up at work. We'll send him a postcard from Spain every day."

On Wednesday, Susan and Carrie headed out the door with suitcases and a bag brimming with presents for their Spanish friends. As usual Mike was perched in Carrie's backpack, his head just high enough to see above the flap.

In the line at the airport, the security guard told Carrie to put her backpack through the X-ray scanner. She placed it in the plastic container but removed Mike first.

"The toy, too," ordered the guard.

"TOY!" said Mike indignantly.

"Here we go again," thought Carrie.

"Behave, Mikey," Susan whispered.

The guard gave Susan a curious look. "Odd," he thought, "Mikey is a funny nickname for a daughter."

"Do I look like a toy?" said Mike to the guard. "You think that I'm battery operated or a wind up? I'm totally not going through that X-ray thing. It could make my moose bones brittle."

Carrie nonchalantly slid her hand over his mouth while Mike continued a muffled protest. She needn't have worried since the guard couldn't hear him. Only a few humans could.

"He prefers not to be X-rayed," said Carrie to the surprised guard. "Could you do a hand search?"

The guard assumed Carrie was kidding, but decided to play along and smiled.

"Why sure, young lady. I'll check him by hand," he said, squeezing Mike like a melon.

"Hey," yelled Mike. "Let go of me. Police brutality!"

The guard heard nothing and holding Mike upside down by the leg, handed him back to Carrie.

"Carrie!" Mike huffed in protest.

"He's just doing his job, Mikey," Susan said.

"Not very well," muttered Mike.

Soon they were seated on the plane with Mike the Moose comfortably propped on Carrie's lap.

The fasten seat belts sign illuminated with a double ding.

"Ladies and gentlemen, please fasten your seat belts," requested the flight attendant, holding up a belt to demonstrate how it fastens.

Mike looked at Carrie.

"I'll slip you under my belt," she said.

"But moose do not wear belts."

"It's for safety," Carrie explained.

Mike shook has antlers to say, no, as, in preparation for departure, the pilot spooled up the jets. Their loud roar rattled Mike.

"You know, I supposed a belt might be fashionable," he said trying to act nonchalant. He hurried to Carrie who helped him fit under hers.

"I do look great in one, don't I."

Carrie smiled.

"What's the delay?" asked Mike as the plane followed others in the departure line.

"It's not our turn yet. The other planes go first," said Susan, leaning over to Mike.

A flight attendant walking the aisle did a double-take. "Tell me that mom isn't chatting with her kid's toy?" she wondered.

After takeoff, Mike watched out the window as the buildings and trees grew smaller.

Moments later, he hard: Ding, Ding.

"Folks, Houston Center advises we'll be hitting a bit of turbulence. Kindly fasten your seat belts, please," the pilot announced.

"Turbo-what? Wuummmph!" Mike said as the plane dropped several hundred feet. His tummy flipped as if on a roller coaster.

Passengers nearby clutched armrests.

Carrie's Pepsi splashed Mike.

Abruptly the plane stopped its descent.

"Next time I want to fly first class," huffed Mike. "They don't have bumps in first, you know."

The plane hit another downdraft and Carrie held Mike tighter.

"Mom, ring the button for the flight attendant please," said Mike. "I'm getting slammed around again. This is the worst job of piloting ever. I want to see proof that the captain has a valid license," said Mike. "Buffie the Bat can fly smoother than this."

"Mikey, remember the *Discovery Channel* show? How the air moves in currents that the plane hits…like a boat in rough waves? The captain can't help that," Carrie explained.

"Buffie doesn't hit waves," insisted Mike.

"But we're at a higher altitude."

"There's nothing wrong with Buffie's attitude, Carrie. The problem is with Captain Kirk up front."

They presented passports at the custom's station where a friendly immigration officer jokingly asked Carrie if her moose had a passport too. It was the wrong thing to say. Now Mike demanded his own passport.

Carrie tried to sidestep Mike's complaints, explaining that customs doesn't require mooselings to carry passports when held in their sister's arms.

"It's discrimination against four legged travelers," insisted Mike. "You have a passport, Carrie. Mom has one. I don't even get my picture taken. I'm writing the Department of Transportation and the Surgeon General's office," said Mike, stamping his hoof.

"Surgeon General?" Carrie questioned under her breath, but softly so Mike wouldn't hear.

Mike wanted to ride on the luggage carousel, but Susan wouldn't have it. They got their suitcases and left to hail a cab.

"Hotel Colon Imperial," Susan instructed the driver.

The ancient yellow taxi sped off, dark smoke belching from the tail pipe as they moved along Madrid's crowded streets.

The cab stopped for a red light next to a tall man in a tan suit who stood at the crosswalk. He looked up as if expecting them, approached, opened the rear door and entered. He nodded to the cab driver who sped forward before the light turned green.

"Driver stop. Right now! Don't you see this man?" yelled Susan, while reaching for the door handle. "Get him out. This is my cab."

"Who is this guy, Mom?" Carrie yelled.

Susan tried to open the door, but the man locked it.

"Susan," said the man. "Susan Grossman. I am not going to hurt you. Let go of the door, please."

"9-1-1. National Guard! Policia. Hellllp," yelled Mike the Moose, though only Carrie and Susan heard him.

"Who told you my name?" said Susan still tugging at the door.

Carrie squeezed Mike.

"Mrs. Grossman," said the man, facing her. "Susan Grossman. Please wait. Just a minute. I'm a friend. I'm here from the U. S. State Department, and I'm not going to hurt you. We're meeting this way because no one else must know. Because America needs your help badly."

"What are you talking about, and again, how do you know who I am?" demanded Susan. "I want him out of my cab, driver."

"I'm Agent Harry Ellis Malone," explained the man, opening a black wallet and flashing a gold badge with his picture ID. Above the badge were the words: U.S. Department of State. And below: Special Intelligence Division.

"He doesn't look especially intelligent to me," Mike said.

"Mike!" Carrie hushed him.

"Ah, no Miss. I'm not Mike. The name is Harry. Special Agent Harry Malone."

"Driver?" said Susan. "Are we being kidnapped?"

The driver turned his head. "No Ma'am. This really is Agent Harry Malone, head of the U.S. State Department in Madrid. I'm a State Department officer too. Agent Cliff Davis."

"What could the State Department possibly want with us?"

"This meeting was set up so I could meet you, Susan, without the others in my office knowing. I have a lot to tell you," said Agent Malone. "But in brief, your country needs your assistance.

"Me? You've got to be kidding."

"You," Malone confirmed.

Susan shrugged her shoulders looking doubtful.

"You are the spitting image of a woman named Margarita Melagrosa De la Rosa Gustamante," Agent Malone said. "That name means nothing to you, I'm sure."

"Maritta Rosa whatchamacallit?" Mike turned to Carrie.

"You look amazingly like her. We found you with face recognition software. Even better, you teach Spanish, which makes it perfect…and that's why we need your help on a top priority, special assignment. A matter of national security."

"I'm on vacation," said Susan. "We're visiting friends who expect us."

"We can't always choose when our country needs us," said Agent Malone looking pious. "Your friends have been contacted. They no longer expect you."

"But I'm just me. Susan. Me and my daughter Carrie. We're not agents. What can we do? And who is the woman you think I look like?"

"I'll fill in the details this afternoon. But the short version is this: we need you to visit the office of an important local official and retrieve information. They'll give it to you as long as they believe you are the real Margarita Melagrosa De la Rosa Gustamante. I can train you to pull it off."

"But, but…what about Carrie?" Susan protested.

"And me?" said Mike the Moose, standing extra tall on his hoofs.

Malone looked only at Carrie.

"It's my country too," said Mike, proudly holding hoof over heart.

"Mike," Susan said, "hold off. This isn't the time."

Agent Malone looked puzzled, wondering, "Why do they keep calling me Mike?" He scratched his head. "Surely they're not addressing the doll Carrie's holding. Of course not. Maybe Carrie still talks to dolls, but Susan's a grown woman. Maybe it's a recorder toy shaped like a moose?"

"Ah, it's Malone, Ma'am. Not Mike," said Agent Malone. "Harry Malone. Is that a recording device?" he asked pointing to Mike.

"Oh no. He's our mooseling." Carrie smiled, knowing Malone would never understand.

"Your….mooselet?"

"Mooseling. My brother…a mooseling," Carrie corrected. "A family member."

"Ah huh," said Agent Malone scratching his head. "Nice, ah, a mooseling. Say, our records show you're nine years old, Carrie That's right, isn't it?"

"I'm seven," said Mike.

"Hush Mike," said Susan.

Now it was agent Malone who wanted to get out of the taxi.

"I'll have to talk to my husband about this." said Susan. "He expects a call from me."

"We've already explained to your husband that you have been detained. He's not classified to get details, but Stephen says he's on board with our mission, if you are. I'll let you speak to him on a secure line from my office, not a cell phone. But you are not free to discuss details, not even with Stephen. It's for your own good."

Susan looked confused.

"Before we go to your hotel, we're headed to the State Department's offices in downtown Madrid. Ambassador Melvin Goodings is in town and wants to brief you. He'll verify what I've said. But except for the Ambassador and Agent Davis here, you are to speak to no none about this. For your own protection Susan, and that goes for you, too, Carrie. If anyone else, even Ambassador Goodings' secretary asks, Susan, you are a reporter doing an article for *US World View*," said Agent Malone. "Can you remember that?"

"I suppose," said Susan.

"Can you remember not to speak a word of this to anyone, Carrie?" asked Agent Malone.

"If Mom says so," said Carrie.

"Okay, we'll speak to no one until I know more about what's going on," said Susan.

"I can keep a secret, Mom, but what about you-know-who here? Mister Blabber Moose," whispered Carrie.

"This is one time that I'm especially glad people can't hear you, Mike," Susan said.

They barely felt the taxi's tired air-conditioning as the Madrid sun beat through the windows. Mike, a cold-weather creature, feared he would wilt. His proud antlers drooped. Carrie's t-shirt stuck to her back, and Susan, eying her lipstick in the taxi's mirror, saw her mascara had run. The dark circles around her eyes made Mike giggle.

"What?" Susan asked him.

"You look like Rudy Raccoon," laughed Mike.

The taxi pulled up to a gated compound with an American flag and the yellow and orange flag of Spain. A marine in a neatly-pressed uniform stepped from the guard booth and peered in.

"Sir." The soldier saluted Agent Malone.

Malone pointed to Susan and Carrie. "They're with me."

"Me, too," insisted Mike the Moose. "I'm with them, which means I'm with him," explained Mike to the solder who couldn't hear him.

"Not now, Mikey," said Susan.

Agent Malone looked worried again.

The taxi circled a fountain with a statue of Christopher Columbus at the entrance. Agent Davis held the door open at the building's main entrance.

"Take their bags to my office," said Agent Malone to a waiting soldier. "Susan, Carrie, please join me," he said, ushering them through the big brass door to a marble hallway.

Large wall clocks displayed the time in major world cities while data scrolled across a computer screen as they entered Agent Malone's office. Piles of papers were unevenly stacked on his desk. Susan noticed Agent Malone's photographs. In one he stood stiffly next to the President; in others he shook hands with dignitaries. Mike liked the picture of Agent Malone in front of a World War II airplane. There was also a photo of Agent Malone with his arm around a little girl.

Carrie's eyes fixed on a poster-sized black and white photograph of a woman that lay on Agent Malone's desk. She nudged Susan and pointed. Susan's eyes widened. Except for a difference in clothing styles, it was astounding how much the woman and Susan looked alike.

"Care for a cold drink?" Malone asked.

"That would be great," replied Mike the Moose. "Carrot juice. On the rocks, please."

"Yes, please," smiled Carrie, shoving Mike down into her backpack. "Could I have a Coke, Mr. Malone?"

"Is there orange juice?" Susan asked.

Malone reached into a small refrigerator. "This okay?"

"Better than okay," said Susan. "My tongue feels like a sand dune."

Agent Malone handed Carrie a Coke.

"What am I, chopped liver?" demanded Mike. "What about me?"

Carrie gently slipped the backpack flap over his head and muffled Mike's complaints. But only Carrie and Susan heard.

Agent Malone started the briefing with small talk. Like Susan and Carrie, he lived in Washington D. C. Finally, when the conversation lulled, Agent Malone held up the photo of the woman.

Susan shook her head. "I feel like I'm looking at myself, Agent Malone. There are a could of small differences if I look closely. My nose is slightly less pointed. Her hair is darker. But otherwise she totally could be me."

"She really could be you, Mom," echoed Carrie.

"You're way better looking," said Mike, popping up again.

"Now you understand why we need you and you alone for operation Data Grab," said Agent Malone. "You are critical"

"Mom's hardly ever critical," said Mike.

"Mike, shhhh," said Susan, forgetting herself.

Agent Malone was about to ask who this "Mike" was, but instinct told him not to. He wanted to be sure of Susan and of her commitment to the mission. But he thought, "it sure seems like both of them talk repeatedly to someone who isn't there. Weird and more than a little worrisome."

Malone rubbed his chin thoughtfully and moved on.

"We have recently learned that several top Inter-Mundo Agents have been repositioned to Spain and are in place to harm American interests. For your own protection, I won't give you more details than you absolutely need. We know their leader, Generalissimo Alfonso Ramonito Crakov del Buston, has a list of every Inter-Mundo agent involved in their plot. Getting that list is vital. The woman you look like," Malone held up the picture of Margarita Melagrosa De la Rosa Gustamante, "was once the General's secretary. Now she is his lover."

Carrie blushed.

"Sorry, Carrie," Agent Malone mumbled. "Indelicate of me, I suppose."

"How about some delicacies for me?" demanded Mike. "At least carrot juice?"

Carrie and Susan ignored Mike.

"But if she's his, ah, girlfriend," said Susan, "surely the General will know I'm not Margarita when he sees me? He'd know his own lover."

"Yeah and my Mom can't date this General guy," said Mike. "She's married to my dad."

"The General would know, of course," said Agent Malone not hearing Mike. "But the way we've planned it, he will never see you. Only the General's staff will see you, and with proper training, we think you can dupe his aides. What matters most is that you fool the General's second in command, Captain Jorge del Pogo.

"You *think* I can pass for her? And if I don't?" Susan looked worried. "What happens to me then?"

"You *will* fool him. The plan is for you to learn Margarita's every habit until everything about her is second nature; how she smiles, how she walks, what she eats, when she sleeps, the words she favors, what she reads. We'll teach you everything you need to deceive del Pogo. And when you have Margarita's mannerisms down pat, we wait until the General goes out of town. Then we act. Our plan is to divert the real Margarita Melagrosa De la Rosa Gustamante and to send you in her place. You'll go to the General's office and download the list of his agents from his computer. With that information, the U.S. will be able to shut down the entire Spanish Q3 network. The lives of many American agents will be saved."

Susan looked unsure.

"You can do it, Susan. We'll train you," said Agent Malone.

"Whoa. Way too risky," said Mike the Moose shaking his antlers atop Carrie's backpack. "Going to the General's office? Too dangerous for me and Carrie and especially for Mom. Now Agent Malone…I believe we'd be willing to do some surveillance for you…say a stakeout by the hotel pool? You know, slyly holding a Carrot Juice Collada and peering through the paper umbrella."

"But what do I tell my husband?" said Susan, ignoring Mike. "Stephen will wonder if we're safe."

"With your okay," said Malone, "our agent in Washington will brief Stephen further this afternoon. We'll let him know you've been delayed to help the State Department and that our best agents in Spain will be devoted to keeping you safe. We cannot tell him more than that."

"What about my safety? Who's devoted to me?" Mike demanded.

"Of course your safety is important, Mike," said Susan.

Susan turned to Carrie. "I can do this. Don't worry."

"Amm…uh…I guess we'll be okay, Mom," said Carrie."

Susan reached into Carrie's backpack and cradled Mike's cheeks softly.

Agent Malone stared. "Should he say anything?" he wondered. "Girls talk to their dolls; my own daughter Wendy does." He smiled looking at Wendy's photo. "But she is younger than Carrie. And what's with Susan interacting with Carrie's doll? Oh, man," he worried, "please don't tell me I'm betting a critical mission on a grown woman who talks to dolls?" Malone waved off the thought. "Too preposterous."

Next morning the sunlight streamed through the floor-to-ceiling windows of their room at the Hotel Calon and threw a sun-rainbow on the wall. Carrie stretched in bed ready for a day of fun after a great night's sleep. She lifted Mike the Moose to her face.

"Morning Mikey. Isn't this outstanding," she said, kissing the end of his pointy moose nose. "Muy bueno, Señor Mike." she said, practicing Spanish she'd learned from her mother.

"Let's stay in bed and watch TV the whole day," said Mike, not eager for intense heat on his delicate antlers again.

"The TV's in Spanish," said Carrie.

"Oh yeah," said Mike. "Maybe they have American channels?"

Susan came in and reminded them that they had other plans.

"We can't go to the pool," she said. "Remember? I start my training with Agent Malone."

For Carrie it was like recalling a bad dream.

"Oh," she said. "I forgot. This trip was supposed to be fun. Couldn't we tell Agent Malone you want to take the day off and start tomorrow?"

"I'm so sorry," said Susan. "I'm totally up for a day by the pool. But the State Department needs our help. We want to be good Americans. And you have to admit; it's pretty amazing how much that woman and I look alike."

"Do I look like her too?" asked Mike.

"Of course not," said Carrie.

"But we still need you, Mikey. We need the support of a strong man, ah, a really strong moose," Susan said.

Mike stood taller.

"You and Carrie can play while I'm training."

"Maybe it won't be so bad," thought Mike, reaching for his marble sack.

Susan poured steaming coffee from the silver pitcher on the breakfast cart wheeled in by the hotel staff. The cart also held crunchy, hot rolls and jellied pastries served on colorful china. There was British Marmalade, a heaping bowel of fresh fruit, and even a vase with red roses.

"Just another typical breakfast like you serve us every day, huh, Mom?" said Carrie.

Susan laughed, "I suppose you'll want silver service when we get home."

"I'd settle for hot chocolate this good," said Carrie.

Precisely at 8:35 A.M. a black Ford Taurus pulled up to the hotel's side entrance. The driver, Agent Cliff Davis again, held the door open.

"Good morning," he smiled. "Agent Malone is set for you."

They sped off through crowded alleyways as the cool morning turned into another sweltering day in Madrid.

Agent Malone stood up politely.

"Was breakfast satisfactory?" he asked.

"Thanks, Agent Malone. It was great," said Susan. "The Hotel Colon is very nice."

"Please call me Harry, both of you. We'll be spending quite of a bit of time together. You're well-rested too, Carrie?" he asked.

"Yes, thank you."

"We should get started," said Agent Malone.

"What am I, a leftover empanada?" asked Mike, popping up from Carrie's backpack. "I slept well too if you must ask," he muttered.

"Not now, Mikey," said Carrie.

Agent Malone no longer bothered to correct Carrie. She never got his name right. "Why should we wait, Carrie?"

"Oh no, Sir; we can start anytime."

Agent Malone was confused. "Very well. Susan, would you please walk for me?"

Susan looked puzzled.

"Walk across the room, please," instructed Agent Malone.

Susan walked back and forth.

"Too prim," said Agent Malone.

Susan had no idea what he meant.

"Watch this please," he said.

He flicked a switch and a screen lowered from the ceiling. On the screen the woman who looked stunningly like Susan came out of a restaurant and walked down the street. She moved gracefully yet with a great deal of movement in her hips, one step rolling into the next like a lioness.

"More like this?" asked Susan, crossing the room again. This time her hips rolled gracefully.

"Yes, yes, Susan. That's much more like her," said Agent Malone, clearly impressed.

Carrie gave Susan a thumbs up.

"Mom!" protested Mike the Moose, embarrassed to see his mom walk that way.

They spent the rest of the morning watching film clips of Margarita Melagrosa De la Rosa Gustamante. There were clips of Margarita eating, dancing, arguing, applying makeup, getting in and out of cars, sitting and standing. Every imaginable movement had been captured on video. Carrie and Mike had to agree when Agent Malone told Susan how quickly she was learning Margarita's mannerisms. In their spare time Carrie occupied herself by drawing pictures on her iPad, but Mike was bored to his antlers.

The afternoon was devoted to makeup – going over the brands of cosmetics Margarita used, showing Susan how she applied lipstick and how heavily she darkened her eyebrows. A colorist came in and dyed Susan's hair to a perfect matching shade.

Mike complained he had nothing to do until Carrie had the colorist take a small section of fur in the middle of his chest and color it – ever so lightly. When the colorist finished, Mike spent the remainder of the afternoon going from mirror to mirror, admiring himself, and talking to an imaginary *Peoples Magazine* interviewer about his new look.

"Image is everything," Carrie heard Mike explaining as he shifted positions in the mirror.

Malone showed films of Margarita with her friends and associates. In one of them Margarita was seated with the General in his private box at the theater. In another she sipped sangria with the General at their usual table at *Café del Jardin*. The General was shorter than Susan had expected for so important a man. The little Turkish cigars he puffed kept his head in a constant cloud of smoke and when he talked, smoke spilled out of his nose like a waterfall. Mike the Moose insisted smoke came out of the General's ears and nose.

"He's like a Chinese dragon," laughed Mike.

"I don't like him," said Carrie.

The General had dark, puffy eyes and heavily greased hair. He rarely spoke when he entered a room, but the eyes of his men always followed him, searching for a hint of anything they could do to please him. He was not a handsome man but one thing was for sure, the general was in charge.

Susan shared Carrie's instant dislike of him and was glad that their paths would not cross. "If I ever see him," she thought, "my biggest challenge will be to hide my dislike."

Agent Malone assured Susan she would not meet the general; she would be long gone and back in America by the time the General returned from his trip.

Mike didn't hesitate to add his own description of the General. Mike called him General Toad Face. This made Carrie giggle but puzzled Agent Malone who couldn't imagine why every time he said the General's name, Carrie laughed.

"I like Margarita's looks," Mike said to Carrie, "and I really, really like Margarita's big gray Abyssinian cat, Imelda. Will I get to meet her, Carrie?"

"Sorry, Mikey," said Carrie. "You won't be crossing paths with Imelda. And we'd better not run into Margarita."

"If we do, we won't be sharing tea," said Susan overhearing Carrie.

Susan trained for another week of long daily sessions until Agent Malone announced, "Susan, you have done brilliantly. You're ready. Operation Data Grab is good to go."

Susan paled. "Are you sure, Harry?"

"Susan, you do Margarita better than Margarita does Margarita."

"But what about the General's travel plans? Don't we have to wait 'til he's out of Spain?"

"The General will be in Monte Carlo next week visiting General John Louis du Papin, Commander of the French Foreign Legion. The two of them go way back and were college buddies. When they party, they are incommunicado an entire week. So get set for Tuesday. That's when we roll."

Susan frowned. "Maybe we should review the plan again."

"Mom, you so have it down," said Carrie.

Mike nodded his antlers.

"Of course we can, if it makes you feel secure," said Agent Malone. "So next Tuesday we pick you up at the Hotel at 8:35 A.M. sharp. At 8:45, across town, our agent, a waitress at the *Blue Grada Café*, will be in place. Margarita has coffee there every morning. She'll lace Margarita's coffee with a drop of Dragon's Wing tea. It's a powerful sleeping potion that will kick in about the time Margarita gets back to her apartment. She'll be knocked out the whole day. Meanwhile, we intercept the general's limo and switch drivers with our look-alike chauffeur. You'll arrive and take your seat in the limo."

Susan nodded.

"You tell me the rest," quizzed Malone.

"Okay," said Susan. "So Agent Anne Batista stays with Carrie at our hotel until I return. Carrie likes puzzles, so if your agent could bring some, please, it would be great. And maybe she could also bring a few marbles?" Susan winked at Carrie. "I get into the general's limo just as you said, and your driver takes me to the general's compound. The man in charge, Captain Jorge del Pogo, will greet me. He'll think I'm Margarita." Susan's brow wrinkled. "At least he'd better..."

"You will pull it off Susan. I absolutely know you're ready," said Agent Malone.

"I tell Captain del Pogo that the general sent me to get some papers from his study, that the general is anxious for them and I am to bring them to the airport right away. I warn Captain del Pogo that the general will be angry if I'm delayed. Captain del Pogo is sure to call the general to confirm all this. But that's okay, because when he does, his call will be intercepted and diverted to a State Department impersonator who does the general's voice perfectly.

"…and then…?"

"So Captain del Pogo leads me to the general's study where, as soon as he leaves me, I insert this in his desktop." Susan held up a tiny thumb drive. "The program on it will retrieve the files you want and when the screen blinks white, I extract the drive. I also gather a few random papers from the general's desk, doesn't matter which ones, so it appears that they are what I came for. I call Captain del Pogo who will see me back to my limo."

"Perfect," said Agent Malone. "Well done. Give me just a moment. I'll be right back." Malone turned and left.

"Now my part..." added Mike the Moose, "...is that while mom is at the computer, I stand by to be sure no one is coming. Then I…"

"Nope, Mike," Carrie interrupted, "You and I are not going with her. It's too dangerous. We wait for Mom at the hotel with Agent Batista."

"Not the way I see it," said Mike.

"Period. No argument. Our suitcases will be packed and as soon as Mom returns, Mr. Malone takes us to the airport to go home. Right, Mom?"

"Exactly honey."

"No way am I staying behind," whispered Mike the Moose under his breath. "If Mom goes on a mission, so do I."

"Not happening Mikey," said Susan who overheard him. "I am your mother, and I'm not putting either you or Carrie at risk. Besides, you don't think it might be pretty weird if Captain del Pogo sees Margarita Melagrosa De la Rosa Gustamante arriving with a mooseling in her arms? What would Captain del Pogo say about that, Mike?"

Mike had to admit his mom had a point.

Agent Harry Malone returned, noting that Susan was again talking to the toy that Carrie had named "Mike."

"What is with that?" thought Malone. "I've come to admire Susan as her training's progressed. I consider her a level-headed woman. Carrie's bright too. But they have this thing about the toy moose. Nothing in the research they sent points to serious peculiarities. But bringing a doll to Spain and talking to it? A grown woman?" Malone looked out his office window to think it over. He was begging to have a few doubts.

4
~

MIKE AND THE MISSION

Tuesday arrived faster than Susan thought possible. It took her three tries to get her lipstick right, raising the stick ever so high at the middle of her lips but keeping it thin at the ends of her mouth. It wasn't Susan's style – way too thick for her – but it matched Margarita's look. Susan put on the clothes Agent Malone provided, a perfect copy of Margarita's tan skirt with flowers embroidered at the base, and a similar thick, black waist belt. The tan blouse looked just like the one she'd seen in the films.

Carrie liked the broach. Agent Malone brought Susan a replica of Margarita's pin – a gold lizard with emerald eyes, perched on a leaf of silver and gold mesh. Before putting it on, Susan added cotton padding to mimic Margarita's cleavage.

Mike turned away, blushing. "Geez, Mom!"

"Almost ready," said Susan, glancing at her watch and touching her ears with a dash of *Revenge of the Night Lovers*, Margarita's favorite perfume.

Agent Batista arrived, looked over Susan carefully, and adjusted a lock of Susan's hair with a brush.

"Perfect," she said.

"Carrie, I'm off," said Susan, kissing her on the cheek. She gave Mike a cheek squeeze. "With any luck I'll only be a few hours."

"Be careful, Mom," urged Carrie setting Mike on the bed.

"Carrie, do you want the American channel?" said Agent Batista, pointing the remote to the TV.

"I'm coming, Mom," Mike protested. "You need me."

"No way, Mikey," said Susan, working her foot awkwardly into a black stiletto high-heel shoe. "You're staying with Carrie and Agent Batista."

As Susan bent to force her swollen foot into the second shoe, he slipped from the bed and dove into the black knit purse that completed the copy of Margarita's outfit.

Susan never saw him, and glued to the TV, neither did Carrie or Agent Batista.

The brass elevator doors opened and Susan hurried out a side door, avoiding the hotel's main entrance. A black Ford waited with the engine running.

Sitting in the back seat, Susan's finger repeatedly traced the outline of the lizard pin as her new chauffeur, wearing the uniform of a Spanish military officer, sped down one alley and up another. Though early morning, the sun warmed the air rapidly. Susan asked her driver to turn up the air conditioning so her abnormally heavy makeup wouldn't run.

Crunched at the bottom of Susan's black knit purse, Mike wasn't happy. He was hot and Susan's comb had wedged onto his antler. But he suffered in silence, afraid Susan might have the driver turn the car back if he were discovered.

Agent Batista saw that Carrie, bored with the limited number of American channels, had fallen asleep and she gently lifted the remote from Carrie's hand.

Carrie slept for a couple of hours and then awoke, startled, and required a minute to recall where she was.

"Maybe Agent Batista will do a puzzle with Mike and me," she thought.

"Hey Mikey, bet I can get more puzzle pieces in place than you can." Silence. Carrie looked around.

"Oh, Mr. Mike the Moose...come out, come outk wherever you are." Silence.

Agent Batista watched with curiosity, wondering as had Agent Malone if Carrie wasn't a bit old to be talking to dolls or a stuffed moose or whatever that was that Carrie always carried. But Agent Batista had been warned and was told to ignore it.

Carrie looked under the bed. Mike was not there. She called him, pulled down the sheets, searched the room, the bathroom, and even looked down the hallway. Mike was gone. She told Agent Batista who only smiled, then helped her look, but she showed little interest.

"I wouldn't worry about it," she said. "I'm sure you left your toy in Agent Malone's office. We'll find it."

"Call Agent Malone and warn him, please. Right now, Agent Batista. It's more important than you know."

"Harry's rather busy now, Carrie," said Agent Batista. "We're in the middle of a critical mission."

"You don't get it," Carrie said. "I'm worried that Mike's on the mission with Mom."

"You shouldn't worry, dear. We'll locate your plaything later," she said patting Carrie on the head.

"Agent Batista doesn't have a clue." thought Carrie. "She has no idea what Mike is capable of. We're in for it now, and there's no way I can warn Mom. I can't reach Agent Malone, and if I could, just like Agent Batista, he wouldn't believe me."

Carrie paced the room peering out the window and wondering if there was anything at all she should do.

"If Mike did sneak out with Mom, he'll endanger her and the whole operation if he's seen," she considered.

Carrie sat on the edge of the bed, kicking her feet, waiting for the bad news. "It's my fault," Carrie decided. "I should never have let him out of my sight."

The Ford sped from the center of Madrid to the countryside. Susan watched the buildings get smaller and the clothing fashions change from downtown stylish to suburban casual and finally to country plain.

The chauffeur swerved off the highway on to a dirt road and then past small farms until the road narrowed and ended in a tree-lined cul-de-sac. He pulled the Ford next to a double-length, chrome-laden, black limo. A forest of antennas protruded from the limo's massive trunk and atop the front fender was a miniature Spanish flag.

Susan saw that a man in a chauffeur's uniform was seated in the rear of the limo. He was blindfolded, handcuffed, and trying to yell through his taped mouth. Another agent pulled him out and shoved him into the back seat of the Ford, even as he told Susan to switch vehicles and get into the back of the limo. Susan's chauffeur moved to the limo. She noticed that his clothes and features were identical to those of his handcuffed predecessor: same height, same build, and same curly black hair. Her chauffeur even had an identical tattoo – a military crest – on the back of his neck.

"That Malone doesn't miss a thing," she thought. "And the back seat of this limo looks like a hotel lobby."

The limo's windows were framed in Brazilian marbled wood. The seats were red silk with rounded arms like a couch, with red velvet pillows on both sides. A small, glass chandelier hung in the passenger compartment.

"The general's tastes are not simple." Susan smiled.

The chauffeur nodded to her and the limo's enormous engine came alive. The full power of its twelve cylinder, supercharged, turbo-coagulated engine roared, and its dual overhead, synchronized, counter-rotating hydroponic cam shafts thundered with spirit. Gleaming wire wheels spit dust as they hurried away.

It seemed like hours to Susan, but precisely twenty-three minutes later, the limo stopped at a gilded wrought-iron guard house. A short soldier stood at attention, then approached to peer in.

"Small wonder he can move at all," thought Susan, "considering the weight of his medals."

Showing a full set of teeth, he smiled and did a half bow. "Señora."

Susan gave the quick condescending nod she'd rehearsed.

"Well I fooled at least one of them," she thought as the limo pulled up at the main entrance.

Though a chandelier in his limo was a bit much, Susan had to admire some of the general's decor. The classic columns on each level up the marble entrance staircase were impressive. Fountains on both sides showered stone mermaids. At the top, more flags of Spain flew, along-side those of the Spanish Army. It was all Susan could do to appear bored and force herself to look straight ahead.

Captain Jorge del Pogo stepped out at the entrance arch to greet her with a half bow and eyed Susan coldly. The decorations on his uniform included the Cross of the Madonna and the Silver Star of the Battle of

La Coruña, reserved for Spain's most decorated officers. Captain del Pogo smiled insincerely and beckoned to Susan to follow.

"Here comes the first test," thought Susan.

"Always a pleasure, Margarita," said the Captain. "Although your visit is unexpected, I believe?" His black eyes penetrated Susan's.

"The interrogation begins," thought Susan.

"Unexpected? I think not Captain del Pogo. Did you not speak with our general?" she asked, meeting Jorge del Pogo's challenge with her own firm stare.

"I did not," Captain Jorge del Pogo said without a blink, "nor did he say…"

"…had you," Susan interrupted, "you would know the general sent me to retrieve important confidential papers for his meeting with General du Papin. He expects them immediately, and his jet awaits to fly them back to France. I am to bring them to the airport. Without delay."

"No Señora, our general did not call me," said Captain del Pogo forcing a smile, "but do not worry, I shall call him even as I escort you to his study," said del Pogo whipping out his satellite phone.

"No need to escort me, Captain del Pogo," Susan said. "It's not like I don't know the way."

"Oh, I insist," said the captain.

The captain dialed and Susan, having memorized the layout, headed confidently to the general's study. As she made her way, she touched a tiny button on her watch to transmit a signal to Agent Malone's waiting men. The message alerted them to re-route Captain del Pogo's satellite call to the impersonator standing by.

"Speak," boomed the impersonator, perfectly mimicking the voice of Generalissimo Alfonso Ramonito Crakov del Buston.

"My Generalissimo, it is Captain Jorge del Pogo."

"I am interrupted. Why?" thundered the voice like the general's.

"Forgive me, My General, but I am confirming that you sent Margarita to retrieve papers from your study?"

"She has not left with them yet?" demanded the impostor general.

"She just arrived, Sir," said the captain, bowing as if the general could see.

"I want the papers without further delay, Captain," said the impersonator hanging up.

45

"Very good, My General," said Captain Jorge del Pogo to an empty dial tone.

Susan entered the general's study. The walls were the finest rosewood the Bolivian rain forests could offer. A crystal chandelier hung in the center of the room and Persian rugs warmed highly-polished marble floors. Susan went to the general's desk and powered up the computer, keeping her back to the door should Captain del Pogo join her. She slipped the flash drive into the USB port even as she heard him enter.

"Captain del Pogo," she turned, "I am so dry. Ask Lupe to bring me cold water. With ice, if you would," said Susan in a louder than usual voice so the captain didn't hear the click of the enter key. The drive whirled as the general's data was found and the download started.

"Lupe," Captain Jorge del Pogo called and slipped out the study door.

Susan went to her purse having remembered a small detail. She'd forgotten to put on the rimmed reading glasses Margarita would wear.

Unable to contain himself in the hot wool purse another moment, up popped Mike the Moose over the purse rim for a look around. Susan saw him and gasped.

"What are YOU doing here?" she whispered angrily. "Get back down in there and I mean NOW."

Mike was so startled by his mom's tone that he skipped the speech he'd prepared and obediently slid down the purse.

Susan turned back to the desk and sifted through the general's papers, feigning to search for particular documents.

"Your water, Señora," said the captain returning and taking a glass off the maid's silver tray.

Susan bit her lip, as the drive continued to whirl. "He's going to be suspicious if this takes much longer. I need to distract him and buy a little time. Then I'll grab some papers, any papers, and leave."

"I assume you are almost done?" the captain questioned, raising an eyebrow.

The screen flashed white, and Susan turned to Captain del Pogo. "I must be sure that I have everything, of course. You would not want me to rush and bring the general an incomplete set now, would you, Captain del Pogo?"

Susan worried, "How am I going to retrieve the flash drive with the captain staring at me." She shuffled a few papers and stood so her back blocked the captain's view of the computer screen.

"You have them all now?" said del Pogo approaching impatiently.

Mike the Moose decided he could not stand the hot purse one more second and chose that very moment to jump from the purse again. He found himself on a table just behind Captain del Pogo. Susan saw him and shot Mike such an angry look that he tore back to the purse. Her look so unnerved Mike that as he jumped antlers first, he knocked a delicate china ashtray off the table. It shattered loudly on the marble floor.

Captain del Pogo turned to the noise and walked over to investigate. That gave Susan enough time to yank out the thumb drive and click off the computer's power. She walked to the table and snatched up her purse. Captain del Pogo stood over the pieces of broken china, looked confused.

"Lupe," he yelled, "bring a broom."

"I hope Margarita won't mention this to My General," he thought, "but I'll die before I'd ask Margarita not to tell him."

As mad as Susan was at Mike the Moose, his accidental distraction had saved the day. "Very well, Captain," she said, heading to the door with a stack of papers. You really should be more careful with the general's priceless china."

Captain del Pogo looked sick but he held Susan back by her arm and took out his pen.

"I will make note of the papers you're taking," said Captain del Pogo, practically snatching them from her.

"If you must," said Susan impatiently, "but be quick or our general will be even more unhappy."

The Captain recorded the title in his note pad: "*Seasonal Variations of Rainfall on Poppy Fields.*" It seemed an odd choice for so urgent a request, but he handed the papers to Susan who, hips swaying down the stairs, went to the waiting limo. She gave the captain a dismissive nod which nicely matched Captain del Pogo's cursory salute from the stairs.

As Susan settled back in the limo she heard Captain del Pogo's satellite phone ring. She hit the button on her watch but knew the impersonator would not have time to intercept a call to del Pogo.

"Get out of here!" she grabbed her chauffeur's shoulder. "NOW."

As the limo jumped ahead, Susan watched Captain del Pogo in the mirror. He snapped his satellite phone closed, and his face turned pale.

"HALT," del Pogo screamed as the limo moved towards the gate.

"Pretend you don't hear him. Break through the gate if you have to," Susan screamed.

"Floor it, buster," added Mike the Moose who had popped above Susan's purse.

Captain del Pogo pulled his Luger and fired a warning shot in the air. He screamed to the startled entrance guard, "Stop them."

The descending bar at the gate hit the limo and shattered as they raced past the guardhouse.

Captain del Pogo's military jeep, loaded with soldiers, pulled up and he jumped in. Two other jeeps followed, all three in pursuit and firing at the bulletproof limo. Shells tore into the limo's side but its occupants were safe and the limo's fuel tank, reinforced with double bubble kryptonite, was impenetrable.

Susan's chauffeur screamed into his cell phone, "Soldiers after us Malone. Del Pogo knows. Three jeeps following. Call up air support. Get them off our tail."

"ON IT," Agent Malone's voice boomed back. "Hold them off for just a couple more minutes."

When he realized that the bullets ricocheting off the windows were real, Mike the Moose started shouting too.

"This was supposed to be a piece of cake," he yelled indignantly. "There are bullets whizzing by me and my mom. Totally unacceptable. That was not the plan. I'm filing a formal complaint with Malone's higher ups," said Mike as a new round of shells peppered the trunk.

"Get down, Mike," said Susan, trying unsuccessfully to stuff him into her purse.

Susan saw a huge oil tanker pull out from a side street and head towards them. The tanker skidded sideways and stopped just behind her limo, forming a wall that delayed del Pogo's jeeps. The driver of the tanker jumped in the limo and they raced away.

The tanker driver held a black box on his lap.

"Now," the chauffeur nodded.

The tanker driver pushed a red button on the box and a moment later the fuel tanker exploded. The blast blew the tires off two of the jeeps chasing them. But the third jeep with Captain del Pogo managed to dodge the blast, edge around the disabled jeeps, and stay in pursuit.

"One jeep still coming," the tanker driver yelled.

"It's del Pogo. Air support should be seconds away," the chauffeur shouted back.

"I hope so," said Mike. "Mom, that jeep's coming fast."

Susan held Mike close.

Overhead she heard the repetitive rhythm of blades beating air. Through the rear windshield they saw the base of a large, drab-olive chopper lowering. It fired two rockets at Captain del Pogo's speeding jeep. The captain dodged left and the missiles passed on the right, exploding well past the jeep.

"Apache's reached us," the chauffeur reported in his cell phone.

A third wooosh.

Captain del Pogo had the chopper in his gun sight when the Apache's third missile hit. The jeep careened to a dusty halt, completely disabled. The last thing Susan saw out the limo's rear window was Captain del Pogo waving his fist angrily.

Mike turned to Susan, "Furthermore, I'm writing my congressman that Agent Malone put us in harm's way. We could have been poolside today. I will accept nothing less than a full apology from the State Department, the Justice Department, and the Bureau of Fisheries and Wildlife. Not only that..."

Susan gently slid her hand over his mouth. Clearly Mike was warming up.

"This isn't the time or the place, Mikey, and when we get back to the hotel, Mr. Moose, you and I will have a serious talk," she said sternly. She gently shoved Mike back in her purse.

Wiping sweat from his brow, the tanker driver squinted at Susan.

The limo pulled next to the black Ford minutes later. Malone's agents guided Susan to the waiting car. The drugs given to the general's real chauffeur were wearing off, and he looked bewildered as they walked him back to the general's limo. He rubbed his eyes and tried to wake up. Looking around, blinking, he couldn't fathom how the gleaming black limo that he'd polished for hours had gotten riddled with bullet holes and caked with mud.

"The general's going to be very mad with me," he worried, rubbing his eyes even harder.

Agent Malone was waiting outside the hotel with Carrie and the luggage when the Ford pulled up.

"No time to waste," he said, helping Carrie in. "Straight to the airport," he told the driver as he joined them.

"Mom, I was so worried," said Carrie hugging Susan. "And Mike, thank goodness you are okay," said Carrie seeing Mike in her mom's purse. "You can't do that, Mikey. You can't just ignore what Mom says. You made me really mad."

"Sorry about everything, Susan," said Agent Malone. "What a time for the general to call del Pogo. He never does that, you know."

Susan handed the flash drive to Agent Malone. "I hope this has what you need."

Agent Malone slid the drive into a protective metal case. "Great job, Susan. You were terrific."

"So you won't do that again, will you?" said Carrie, talking into Susan's purse.

"He's a very disobedient moose Carrie. Mike, you can consider yourself under house-arrest," said Susan, also speaking into her purse. "Though I have to admit, Carrie, that Mike provided a life-saving distraction, even if he did so by accident."

Susan told Carrie about Mike and the china ashtray.

"I saved the whole mission, Carrie," said Mike, popping up from the purse.

"Good thing you did, Mikey, or you'd be in even bigger trouble than you are now," said Carrie.

Agent Malone looked at Susan. "You know we can never acknowledge what you accomplished today, nor may you ever speak of it. But it's no small service that you performed. The information on this drive will halt the terrorist activities the general has planned. I can't say anything publicly, but at least let me give you this small token from a grateful nation."

He handed Susan a gleaming jeweled pin. It was gold with an American eagle outlined in brilliant diamonds and rubies. "Only a handful of Americans have this. It's the highest secret honor we can give a civilian. What is more…"

"…What is more, I've had about enough of this," said Mike the Moose interrupting. "I've been stuffed in a hot purse, told to hush up, shot at, banged around in a speeding limo…all of this when it was I who distracted Captain del Pogo so Mom got the flash drive…"

"…and…," continued Agent Malone, not hearing Mike's tirade but lifting him out of Susan's purse, "…and we have been talking to your dad, Carrie, and Stephen told us about your little sidekick here. Now I know why your mom kept calling me 'Mike' and talking into Carrie's backpack. I get it now. Well…I sort of do. Anyway for this little guy…I believe you call him Mike the Moose…for him we also have a special honor," he said gently holding up Mike. "We call it the State Department's Special Order for Superlative Moose Service." He handed it to Carrie who gently hung the chain and tiny medal on Mike's chest.

"I liked you all along, Malone," said Mike. "And as I said," Mike added with uncharacteristic modesty, "it was practically nothing. Just something I could do for my country. Saving the entire mission, of course," he noted, brandishing a full row of teeth. His new medal glistened in the sun.

Malone heard nothing but he loved seeing Susan and Carrie smile.

They waited in the executive terminal until the State Department's pilot cleared them to board. With Mike peering over Carrie's backpack, they headed down the long corridor to the tarmac. As they did, a group of men entered at the arrival end. Susan's eyes were drawn to a short man with his head enveloped in a cloud of cigar smoke. His military uniform was loaded with medals. As they drew closer she could just about make out his face. He was surrounded by muscular aides carrying machine guns who scanned the corridor in every direction. As they neared, she heard him barking orders to his aides, then into a cell phone. Susan realized who he was and turned her away, pretending to talk to her pilot so he wouldn't notice her face.

As the two groups passed, Susan's vise-grip was just releasing the pilot's hand when she heard the general's abrupt command: "STOP!"

His soldiers froze in place.

Susan, Carrie and the pilot turned pale, fearing they'd been discovered; that it was over for them.

The General clapped his hands. "My cigars? I'll have my gift from General du Papin." An aid rushed over with a silver box.

"Keep walking," the pilot whispered under his breath.

Susan, Carrie and the pilot sighed simultaneously and continued on.

The State Department's Citation lifted off the Madrid runway. Carrie was busy fanning Mike who'd fainted when he too saw the general. Finally she roused him. He lifted his antlers and looked dazed.

"You were terribly brave, Mikey," Carrie assured him. "Helping Mom... your medal...well, you're awesome," Carrie stroked her brother's antlers.

Mike looked at Carrie and then at the handsome medal hanging from his neck. His smile went antler to antler.

5

MIKE MAKES FRIENDS

Mike the Moose was preoccupied for weeks after returning from Spain. He spent much of his day in front of the tall hallway mirror admiring himself and posing with his shiny medal of mooseling honor. Carrie heard him making speeches, standing on his hind hooves and rambling on.

"The antler is mightier than the sword, Yo," said Mike, and, "Speak softly but carry big antlers," not to mention, "We Mooselings have a dream."

His speeches always ended making the same point, "Ask not what you can do for your country, until you hear how much I did for mine!" Mike delivered his closing line, taking a long low dramatic antler bow.

One afternoon Mike watched the President of the United States hold a press conference on TV.

"I want to hold one," he advised Carrie. "The whole world should know what I did for America."

Overhearing Mike, Susan reminded him that the mission in Madrid was top secret which quieted him for the moment, and he headed back to the mirror.

Mike's attention finally returned to playing in the bedroom with Boris the Bat and Buffie the Giraffe and also to challenging Carrie to video games and marbles. Life at the Grossman home was returning to normal. (Well as normal as things are in a human home with a self-admiring mooseling.)

On a windy morning Susan mentioned that she had a meeting to attend at the nearby orphanage.

"Carrie, Mike, want to come?"

"Sure Mom," said Carrie.

"You bet," said Mike. "What's an orphanage?"

"It's a home for kids without moms and dads," said Carrie. "Children who hope to be adopted."

Mike thought a moment. "Was I in an orphanage before you Dopted me up?" asked Mike.

"Not really. Don't you remember the yard sale? Although I suppose since you were with Oggie and Gaggle and your other friends, it was like an orphanage," said Carrie.

Mike looked worried. "If I go with you to the orphanage, I'm coming back home, right?"

"Of course you are," said Carrie. "Mike you are a member of this family, and we will never, never, ever let you go."

"This is your home forever, Mikey," said Susan.

"So it's just a short visit? 'Cause *The Simpsons* are on at eight," said Mike.

"You'll be home in time," said Carrie.

"'K," said Mike, reassured.

On arrival, Mike felt relieved that the orphanage didn't look like a yard sale. Actually there was hardly any yard at all around the brick building with time-darkened walls and climbing ivy. Carrie remarked that the inside of the building looked old although it was really clean. Sure enough, cracks showed in the highly-polished linoleum, chips dotted the window trim, but the rooms were tidy. Cheery classrooms had rows of pictures done by the children on the walls. Susan and Carrie each toted a bag heavy with toys and clothes collected from a church drive. The congregation had donated new X-Box games, several softballs, a half dozen pairs of neatly pressed jeans, six pairs of Nike sneakers, twelve T-shirts in different colors, a hockey stick, a slightly scraped-up skate board, a *Harry Potter and the Sorcerer's Stone* book, and two pair of plastic binoculars.

A woman at the reception desk wore wire-rim glasses that rested on the end of her rather long nose. She smiled seeing Susan and Carrie.

"Hi, Grossmans," she said, and then noticing Mike peeking out of Carrie's backpack, added, "and may I ask who is this little fellow?" She squeezed Mike the Moose's cheeks, scrunching his mouth as tall as it was wide.

"Let-meee-gooo," Mike demanded through his twisted jaw.

"He's the newest member of our family," said Carrie. "This is Mike the Moose, Master of Marbles."

"And who's the Grinch who stole Christmas?" mumbled Mike pointing to his tormentor. "Let me guess. She's a ninja torture expert sent by Captain del Pogo to get payback."

The woman heard nothing of course and smiled.

"The kids are in the lunchroom," she said. "They'll be thrilled to see you and to meet Mr. Mike the Moose." She laughed, showing a mouthful of bubble gum.

"Humph," muttered Mike the Moose, free at last from her grip. Feeling returned to his jaw.

Mike was still complaining about her as she led them down the hall and into a big room. Thirteen children read books, drew pictures, or played with games at a large table in the center of the room. Three children worked on a big puzzle at another table. The puzzle wasn't completed enough to make out the whole picture, but Mike could see an outline forming of a plump man in a red suit with hints of a long, white beard.

Near the far end of the table stood a rotund woman with huge cheeks. She greeted Susan and Carrie with a welcoming smile.

"Hi," she said, crossing to hug them. "Sure glad to see the likes of you two!"

"Good to see you too, Nurse Claire," said Carrie, giving her a great big hug that lasted too long for Mike who was unceremoniously squished between them.

"Well, kids," said Nurse Claire, "what do we say when Mrs. Grossman and Miss Carrie come to visit?"

"H-e-l-l-o Mrs. Grossman," came a chorus in near unison. "H-e-l-l-o Carrie."

"Hi right back at you," said Carrie, taking gifts out of her sack."

The children watched Carrie; their heads followed each movement like a tennis match.

Nurse Claire gestured to the children who responded on cue.

"Thank you Mrs. Grossman," came their chorus. "Thank you Carrie."

"Kids, I want you to meet someone very special," said Carrie gently lifting Mike. "This is Mike the Moose, Master of Marbles. He's an expert on marbles and knows all about clearies, and toothpastes, and milkies, too. He's my new brother."

Mike bowed and took a few of his most prized marbles from his pouch.

"You kids ought to know marble terms. How many do know?" Mike asked.

The children just stared.

"Terms like 'Knuckle Down,'" Mike continued. "That's the correct hand position when you begin a marble tournament. Do you know 'Quitsies' and 'No-quitsies' – when you can quit a game without penalties and when you can't. 'Keepsies' is really important. You get to keep the marbles that you win. I like playing Keepsies…at least when I win. How many of you know what marbles are made of?"

The children continued to stare.

"They're made of all kinds of stuff," Mike said. "Glass, steel, clay, even agate. Betcha didn't know that marbles came from Pakistan a long time ago. It was the bronze age," Mike added, extending a hoof in the air for emphasis.

A little girl with peach red hair and freckles said, "The bronze age?"

"Wow, Carrie," said Mike, "she hears me. I like that."

"Did you get your marbles playing Keepsies?" asked a boy with a Batman T-shirt, standing at the front of the group.

"I think they can all hear me," said Mike, clapping his hooves.

"Wow," said Carrie. "You're right; they can Mike! But I don't think all children can. The kids at the mall couldn't hear you. Maybe it's an orphan-to-orphan thing?"

Mike looked annoyed.

"I only mean since you used to be an orphan," said Carrie.

"I really like your marbles Mr. Mike Moose," waved a small boy with oversized eyeglasses.

"Aren't they cool?" said Mike, holding up his sack. "Wanna know something else?"

"Tell us, tell us," said a plump boy in jeans with a cowboy hat, seated at the far end of the table.

"I was an orphanage too!" said Mike.

"You were an orphan," Carrie corrected.

"Yeah that," said Mike.

But the boy looked puzzled. "Then how come you came here with them?" he asked, pointing to Susan and Carrie.

"Yeah. How come you don't live with us?" said a little girl with pigtails.

"Well," Mike answered, "one day Mom and Carrie and my dad Stephen came to a yard sale...ah...to my orphanage...and spoke to the lady in charge, and they took me home. I was Dopted up."

"A-dopted, Mike," Carrie corrected.

"Yeah Dopted," repeated Mike. "So now I have a mom and a dad and a sister. Dogs too. Three of them."

The little girl's eyes lowered. "Will I ever get Dopted up?"

"A-dopted," Carrie corrected.

"And me, too," said a little boy wearing a blue baseball cap backwards.

"And me," said a little girl with black braids who held a well-worn book.

"Children," Nurse Claire interrupted to change the subject, "may I remind you about these lovely new toys and clothes."

"But will I get Dopted up?" repeated a little red-haired girl looking very serious. She turned to Susan. "Once a nice couple visited me and told me all about their pretty, red house with flowers. They came back twice, but they never come any more," she said looking down at the floor. "I'll bet if I'd worn a prettier dress..."

"They loved you, Kristin," said Nurse Claire to the little girl. "But I told you. The paperwork...do you remember?"

"Couldn't we have done the paperwork?" asked the little girl.

"Kids, kids," said Nurse Claire, "who wants to try the new X-Box?"

"Carrie," Mike turned, "won't they ever get Dopted up like me?"

"I honestly don't know, Mikey," said Carrie. "I sure hope so."

"Me too," said the girl with black braids.

"We all want to get Dopted up like Mike," said a little girl with braces who hadn't yet spoken.

"Mom," said Mike, "why don't we Dopt them up? My room is big enough. Humpy and Boris don't mind sharing. Right, Carrie?"

"I wish we could, Mikey," said Susan hugging Mike, "but with your dad and I working there's no one home to take care of little children. It's a wonderful thought though."

Mike looked down but then brightened.

"Carrie," he said, "can I play with the kids awhile?"

"Sure," said Carrie, helping Mike up on the table.

"You sure it's okay, Susan?" asked Nurse Claire. "Kids be gentle with Mike the Moose."

"I'm quite durable," said Mike. "I made it through Spain and even an American mall."

The children took turns holding and kissing Mike. Mike decided the children were his BFFs. He had such a great time that he forgot all about his plan to spend the day modeling his medal in the mirror.

In the car on the way home, Mike asked Susan again, "Couldn't we Dopt them up, Mom?"

"We don't have room," said Carrie.

"I can take up less room," Mike offered, curling into a furry ball.

"I'm sorry, Mikey," said Susan.

Mike lit up with an idea.

"Carrie," he said, "I know who can help the kids get parents."

"Who?" said Carrie.

"Agent Malone!" said Mike. "I'll collect what he owes me."

"Collect? What are you talking about Mikey?" Susan said.

"When Agent Malone gave me my medal, he said the country owes us a great debt. So we make him pay up. What if it's enough to buy parents?" said Mike, pleased with his scheme.

"Honey, I don't think Agent Malone meant that the State Department actually owes us money," said Susan. "And what's more, you don't buy parents. Parents have to want children badly…the way Dad and I and Carrie feel about you."

"So why don't they Dopt them up, Mom?" asked Mike.

"They want to Mikey, but it's not that simple. The adoption paperwork takes years. The red tape is wearing everyone out."

"'K," said Mike, puzzled. "But what's tape have to do with it? I'll bet Agent Malone can help. He's a pretty good guy even if he doesn't hear well," said Mike.

Then Mike had another thought.

"Hey Carrie, didn't Agent Malone tell you he Dopted up a little girl? Isn't her name Wendy? So maybe Wendy can hear me since she was an orphan too. Maybe she'll ask her dad to help. Could we call her? As soon as we get home?"

"It's not a bad idea, Mike. But I wouldn't have a clue how to reach the home of a top official like Agent Malone," said Susan.

"Or how to reach his daughter," said Carrie. "I'm sure his address is all hush, hush. You can't just google the whereabouts of top officials," explained Carrie.

"Ezy-breezy Carrie. I memorized the phone sounds when Agent Malone called Wendy at home. Boop beep boop tink tink bomp blink tank blink tank," said Mike mimicking Malone's smartphone. "The tones stand for 202-647-6575. So could you call him, Mom? Will-ya? Will-ya Carrie? Tonight?"

"Mikey, I want the kids to get adopted too, but I don't think there's much Agent Malone can do," said Susan.

"You always say you can't succeed if you don't try Mom. Those kids really want moms and dads," said Mike.

"Well, okay. I don't even know if we are supposed to have contact with Agent Malone. But I guess the worst that can happen is he'll tell us not to call again," Susan said.

After dinner they went to the phone in the study and put it on speaker. Mike called out the numbers and Carrie dialed.

The phone rang unanswered until an answering machine picked up. Agent Malone's voice advised callers to leave a message.

"Hi Agent Malone. It's me, Mike the Moose, of course, and…well…" Mike stopped mid-sentence. "Mom if Agent Malone can't hear me in real life, can he hear my phone message?"

The phone clicked and a small voice came on. "Hi, who are you?" said a little girl.

"Hi who are you?" said Mike.

"Wendy," said the little girl. "Dad's not home. Who are you? You sound little. Are you a kid?"

"Actually I'm very tall – especially with my antlers. I'm famous too… decorated for bravery, you know. I'm Mike the Moose. Your dad must have told you about me. A mooseling. The Master of Marbles," said Mike. "Your dad knows me well. We really, really need his help."

"Oh gee, Mr. Moose," said Wendy, "Dad's not home. What's wrong?"

"It's the kids at the orphanage. They're orphans. All of them. Do you know what that means?

"I think so."

"It means they have no moms and dads because the paperwork to get Dopted is tied up in tape. Everyone needs a mom and dad. Can your dad help us?"

"That's awful," said Wendy. "I know…'cause I'm adopted too.

"Dopted," corrected Mike.

"I'm sure Dad wants to help. As soon as he gets home I'll ask him. Do you have a phone number, Mr. Moose?"

An hour later the phone in the study rang. Agent Harry Malone was on the line, and Susan put the call on the speaker box.

"Hi Susan," he said. "If it was anyone but you, I'd be amazed that you found out my phone number."

"I had help getting it." Susan winked at Mike.

"I can guess," said Agent Malone. "If not from Carrie it must have come from our medal recipient. What's this that Wendy tells me…some kids want my help?"

"Some really nice children could sure use a hand, Mr. Malone," said Carrie leaning towards the speaker box.

"With what, Carrie?"

"Could we possibly meet with you Harry?" said Susan. "For just a few minutes?"

"Well," Agent Malone said, "My schedule is a bit jammed. But I have a meeting in downtown D.C. tomorrow. If you don't mind riding along with me we could talk on the way. That'll give us a half hour, and my driver will take you home. Is that enough time? Can you be ready at, say, 11:30 tomorrow if we pick you up?"

"That would be great, Harry. Thank you so much," said Susan. "We'll be out front at 11:30 sharp."

The next day Carrie slipped Mike into her backpack.

"Here we go again," thought Mike as Agent Malone's black limo pulled in the driveway. The driver held the door.

"Here's the story, Harry," said Susan as the car sped along the beltway. "The kids at the Watertown orphanage need good homes and parents."

"I can appreciate that," said Agent Malone. "You know my Wendy is adopted."

Susan nodded. "And there's a list of qualified couples who want to adopt the children. But the adoption process takes forever because the amount of paperwork is staggering. I promised to help the kids but you're the only important person I know. Can you help us?"

"Me?" said Agent Malone. "I'm State Department, not Social Services. What can I do?"

"Nothing if you don't try," mumbled Mike from the top of Carrie's backpack although Agent Malone heard nothing.

"Hush, Mike!" said Carrie looking peevish.

Malone remembered Carrie and Susan's weird habit.

The phone in the limo rang and the privacy partition lowered.

"The White House, Sir," said the driver.

Malone nearly knocked Mike out of Carrie's backpack in his rush to reach the red phone.

"Agent Malone, here." he replied. "Of course I'll hold for the president."

Carrie noticed how much deeper Agent Malone's voice had turned.

Mike's eyeballs nearly popped when Agent Malone said "the president."

"Mike the Moose, Master of Marbles here," Mike yelled towards the red phone, "the highly decorated winner of the Mooseling Medal of Honor."

Carrie slipped her hand over Mike's mouth, not that Agent Malone could hear him.

"Please, Mike," whispered Susan.

"Yes, Sir," said Malone. "I understand. On the way, Mr. President."

Agent Malone nodded to the driver who exited for the George Washington Memorial Parkway and sped towards the nation's capital.

"Sorry, Susan," said Agent Malone, "I've been called to the White House. I'm afraid you will have to come too. My meetings with the president never last more than a few minutes. You and Carrie can wait outside the Oval Office, if you don't mind."

"No problem, Harry," said Susan. "Actually I'd really like that."

"Cool," said Mike. "I'm summoned to the White House. It's about time. I'm pretty sure the president wants to pin my medal on me himself. There will be a ceremony, no doubt," said Mike waving his shinny medal in the air. "And paparazzi."

The White House was even more awesome than Carrie expected. Susan became solemn walking down the long corridors. Mike wasn't at all in awe; he felt annoyed. The walls were filled with historic documents, portraits of presidents and pictures of great battles. There were sculptures and swords and mementos of America's rich history. But Mike felt the White House corridors were woefully lacking.

"Not one portrait of a moose," muttered Mike. "Do these guys have any idea what moose have contributed to America? We designed the first television antennas, we invented the coat rack, and the Charleston dance was first performed by Uncle Morris Moose whose knees wobbled uncontrollably."

Agent Malone directed them to a comfortable settee across from the Oval Office. Two Marines opened the door and moved aside as Malone entered to meet with the President.

Minutes later, the door to the Oval Office opened and out walked Agent Malone. For a second, Mike could see inside the office, and he even caught a glimpse of the President of the United States seated at his desk. Simultaneously the president looked up and noticed Agent Malone standing with Susan and Carrie, who held Mike. The president arose and the two Marines snapped to attention while another held the door.

"This is your wife, Harry? Never met her," said the president approaching.

"Oh no, Mr. President. This is Susan and Carrie Grossman. Sir, Susan is the civilian who helped us shut down Generalissimo Alfanso Ramonito Crakov Del Buston. Without her, his plot might have succeeded."

The president shook Susan's hand vigorously and Carrie's too.

"I know about operation Data Grab and your great help, Susan," he said. "You're a brave woman. Would you like to step into the Oval Office a minute? And you too, Carrie?"

"It would be a tremendous honor, Sir, if it's not an imposition," said Susan, smiling nervously while contorting her legs into an awkward half-curtsy.

"What about me? I'm the one who made it possible to get the general's data. Am I not invited?" said Mike the Moose.

The president stopped in his tracks. To their utter shock it seemed he could hear Mike the Moose even though most adults and non-orphan children couldn't. The president looked at Mike and smiled at Agent Malone.

"By golly, Malone," said the president, "You weren't kidding. So your reports of a moose with them in Spain were for real? Absolutely you're invited, Mike," said the president, reaching for him. "May I, Carrie?"

Carrie let the president take Mike.

"You can hear him?" questioned Susan. "Most adults can't."

"You hear it, Sir?" asked Agent Malone. He turned a shade paler, surprised that the president could hear Mike since he never could.

"He hears ME," said Mike the Moose. "I'm no IT." Mike turned and gave the president his full teeth smile.

"Of course I hear him. Being president doesn't make you deaf," said the Commander in Chief, "although it would be convenient if I could go deaf when a certain Speaker of the House visits."

"I wonder why some people hear Mike and others can't?" Carrie asked aloud.

The president turned to Mike the Moose. "Look my little friend," he said, "would you like me to show you something no visitors to the White House have ever seen?"

"That'd be so cool, Your Presidency," said Mike the Moose.

The president led them to the Oval Office and set Mike on the Resolute Desk. He opened the bottom left drawer and to Mike's amazement the President of the United States took out a red yo-yo. It bore the presidential seal on both sides.

"Watch this, Mike," said the president, throwing his yo-yo. It spun fast in mid-air, hung suspended a great long time, made a complete swinging circle, and returned to the president's hand.

"Awesome, Your Presidency. You Circled the World. Wow," said Mike. "You like that, Mike, well watch this." The president took off his suit jacket, rolled up his shirt sleeves and pulled something else out of the drawer. This time he released two yo-yos and did the trick with two hands at once.

"Go Pres," cheered Mike, until he caught the stern look from Susan. "I mean, quite wonderfully done Your Presidency," said Mike, eyes wide.

The president laughed, and holding Mike in his arms, sat on one of the couches in the Oval Office, motioning that Susan, Carrie and Malone should join him.

The president's private secretary entered.

"Begging your pardon, Mr. President, but the Secretary of the Treasury is waiting in the Green Room."

"Won't be long," said the president. "So Mike, Carrie and Susan," he asked, "how is it that you're here with my top State Department agent?"

"Well, Mr. President," Susan explained, "we were asking for Agent Malone's help. We often visit the children of the Watertown orphanage. The kids need us and we want to support them.

"How so?"

"A lot of really good people want to adopt them, Sir, but the amount of red tape involved overwhelms them. The process drags on and on. We asked Harry, ah Agent Malone, if there was any way he could help expedite the adoption process."

"It is a wonderful cause, Mr. President, "said Agent Malone "but I don't know why Susan asked me. I don't have Social Services contacts."

"I might have a few," said the president. "Susan, would you mind if I stuck my two cents in? Carrie, is that okay?"

"Mr. President would you! Oh please, do Sir," said Carrie.

"They are great kids who badly want and need good parents," said Susan.

"That'd be awesome," said Mike.

The president went to his desk and asked his personal secretary to get someone on the line for him. He spoke for several minutes. Mike heard him say 'adopted' repeatedly and was about to correct him when the president spoke.

"I suspect that will help," said the president, putting down the phone.

They arose and thanked the president for his time. Susan did another twisted curtsy. Carrie smiled. But the president hardly noticed. He was slipping something to Mike, and he put a finger to his lips – to signal Mike it was a secret.

Susan was in a daze on the ride home. Carrie too. They had just met and even chatted with the President of the United States – in the Oval Office! Even Mike the Moose was quieter than usual. Mike held tight to his new gift – a handsome red yo-yo that bore the seal of the President of the United States of America.

The phone rang a week later. It was Nurse Claire from the orphanage. "Can you come quickly? You've got to see this, Susan. Hurry," she urged.

Susan pulled into a parking space at the Watertown orphanage. Carrie grabbed Mike and hurried in, waving as they dashed past the receptionist. Nurse Claire stood down the hall, eager to usher them into the playroom.

The room glowed with happiness. Moms were brushing kids' hair, gently tucking in their shirts, cleaning eyeglasses, blowing noses, and there was a lot of hugging. Every child had a parent; some even had new brothers and sisters. Parents beamed and many of the kids simply held hands with their new mom and dad, or their dad and dad or their new mom and mom.

"May I have your attention, new parents?" Nurse Claire clapped for silence. "I'd like to introduce the people responsible for your adoptions – for getting the red tape cut."

Mike popped over Carrie's backpack and started bowing.

"The word is Doption," he corrected Nurse Claire. "And to be fair, the president helped too."

"Kids and new parents," continued Nurse Claire, turning to Susan, "meet the women who made this possible – the Grossmans: Susan and her daughter Carrie."

"The women!" said Mike exasperated. "Do I look like a woman?"

The kids laughed although Nurse Claire and the parents couldn't hear Mike.

"Hi Kids," waved Susan. Carrie waved too.

"Yo," said Mike the Moose giving them a hi-hoof.

Every child had an ear-to-ear smile.

Every Dad had an ear-to-ear smile.

Every Mom had an ear-to-ear smile.

New brothers and sisters had ear-to-ear smiles.

Susan and Carrie had ear-to-ear smiles.

Nurse Claire's smile was ear-to-ear too.

But the antler to antler smile belonged to Mike the Moose, because nobody understood better then he, how happy the children were.

6

~

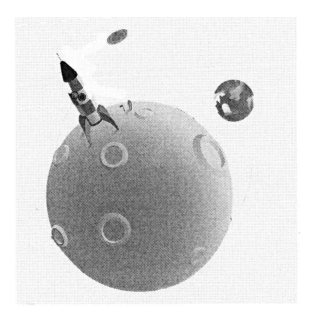

MIKE GOES GALACTIC

Days when Carrie was in school were boring for Mike, not a lot to do except watch the dogs scratch and hear them noisily slurp from their kitchen bowls.

"What do you expect of dogs," muttered Mike, eying the trail of water. Mike had asked if he could go to school too but was told that mooselings weren't allowed. That prompted his cry for legal representation and a demand to address the full school board and the ASPCA, until Susan calmed Mike with her plan to homeschool him. Homeschooling, she explained, would involve an extensive study of marble-making through the ages. Mike agreed it was the most important subject. Now he wanted nothing less than home-schooling.

Mike's marble knowledge grew.

"Do you know, Carrie, that the word marble comes from a Greek word that means "shining stone?" asked Mike, raising his moosebrows and sounding professorial.

"Ummm, that so," said Carrie, thumbing her smartphone.

"And Roman kids played with marbles too?"

"That so," said Carrie.

"And there's a World Championship for Marbles every year in England. Hey, I could go. Couldn't I? Carrie? Could I?"

"Huh," said Carrie looking up. "'Spose so. But the games are probably for the biggest names in the world of marble players."

"Exactly why I need to be there," said Mike.

"We'll see, Mike," said Carrie.

Saturday was Mike's favorite day of the week since Carrie was home. Carrie said she wanted a few more minutes in bed before helping Susan make breakfast and fold the laundry. She lingered with Mike in her arms, and the two of them warmed in the sunlight that streamed through the windows. It felt good on Mike's antlers, but he was getting restless.

"This is really nice," said Carrie.

"But let's go do something," Mike said.

Eddy, the big black lab, arrived and tugged on the bed sheet, eager like Mike for the day to start.

Carrie pulled the covers off just as Mike's patience gave out.

"So Carrie, what's the plan?" he said, putting his snout to Carrie's nose.

"Gee Mikey, I don't know. What are you up for?"

"We could watch the *National Geographic* moose video again. Or go ice skating? Or play with our X-Box?"

"Yeah," said Carrie, "or we could see Spider-Man. Mom said she'd drive us to the Cineplex."

The phone in the living room rang, and they heard Susan answer it.

"Yes, this is Susan Grossman. Yes, 43 Bell Air Drive in D.C. Well, of course, I remember Agent Harry Malone. Of course, I'll take his call. It's Agent Malone," Susan whispered as Carrie and Mike entered the living room.

"We're just fine, thank you, Harry. And you and Wendy?" asked Susan.

"Mom! Mom!" Mike was jumping on four hooves as if the living room rug was a trampoline. "THE Agent Malone? From Spain and the White House? Wendy's dad?"

Susan nodded.

"Air tickets? And a free hotel? It won't cost a thing! As guests of the President. Honoring civilian heroes. For real, Harry? Us? Of course, we accept. Of course, we can be ready," said Susan. She winked at Carrie. "No, sadly, Stephen can't come because he's in San Francisco. He's speaking at a convention. But Carrie? Of course, she wants to come, Sir."

Carrie nodded vigorously.

Susan jotted down some flight numbers.

"Thank you so much, Harry. What a wonderful opportunity. Please let the president's personal secretary know how very grateful we are," said Susan. Then very quietly and with her back to Mike so he couldn't see her, Susan whispered, "Bye for now, Harry," and she pressed the button to end the call. But with Mike watching, she pretended to continue the conversation.

"Mike the Moose too, Harry? Why, thank you, Harry, but I doubt that he'd want to go to Florida."

Carrie, knowing her mom had already hung up, started laughing.

"Florida!" cried Mike doing somersaults on the rug. "I *do* want to go. I do, I do. The snow outside is for penguins. I want to listen to my iPod by the pool and wear my orange shirt with the palm trees. I want sun and coconut juice and..."

"Shhh, Mikey," said Carrie, playing along, "How can Mom hear Agent Malone?"

"But I want to go to Florida too," said Mike.

"Gee Harry, I don't know," said Susan, still pretending. "My schedule is clear. Carrie says she's free. But give me a moment to ask Mike the Moose if he wants TO VISIT NASA AND SEE THE FIRST MANNED MARS MISSION LAUNCH. That wouldn't be too dull for you, would it, Mike?"

Mike fell back on the floor, hooves waving wildly over his belly.

"NASA. The Mars launch! Tell Agent Malone I'll be there, Mom. Oh and you and Carrie may come too!" he said magnanimously.

"Well, Harry," said Susan with mock seriousness, "it seems that Mike the Moose has had a change of heart. His schedule may be free after all to attend the Mars launch and meet THE DIRECTOR OF ALL OF NASA.

Mike was skidding on the rug like it was ice.

Carrie had mercy and lifted him in her arms.

"This is incredible Carrie. We get to go to NASA and see astronauts and the Mars Launch. I can't believe it," said Mike. "Next to marbles I love outer space."

Suddenly Mike grew serious: he put a hoof to his forehead in a salute. "This is historic, Carrie. A mooseling shall witness America's triumph, a vessel carrying men to the stars...to Mars..."

Susan googled the planets and pointed to Mars, hoping to distract Mike from another speech. "It's the fourth planet out from the sun," she said. "And I didn't know you were so poetic, Mike."

"Oh yeah, Mom. Besides the dozens of speeches I've written," said Mike. "I compose poems too. I'm known for my *In Praise of Antlers*. And you gotta hear my *Haiku to a Moose's Mane*. Of course *Ode on a Grecian Marble* is my best known work." Mike waved his hooves dramatically and began:

> *"I think that I shall never see,*
> *a thing so bright as my new clear-y."*

"Yes, yes," said Susan, rolling her eyes, "perhaps we can hear the rest later. But now we have to pack," she added. "And I've got to call your father and tell him. I wish he could join us...but you know your dad's work schedule. He's the main speaker at the conference he's attending, but he'll be disappointed that he can't join us."

"I really wish he could come," echoed Carrie.

"Tell Dad that I promise to tell him everything about NASA," said Mike.

"He'll appreciate that Mikey," said Susan.

"And Carrie could you pack my blue sweater with the gold 'M' please?" said Mike.

Carrie could see an idea forming in Mike's mind.

"Because if you could cover the last line of the 'M' it could look like the 'N' in 'NASA?' And of course I'll wear my medal from Spain with it and..."

Carrie gently cut Mike short with a kiss on his snout. Mike smiled as he watched her pack the suitcase so full it could pop.

The flight south was without incident until Mike ordered a Frosty Whip cone from the flight attendant. Like most people, she didn't hear him. When Carrie explained they didn't have Frosty Whip at 40,000 feet, Mike decided the airline's service was inferior. He kept insisting to speak to the airline's CEO until finally over North Carolina, he fell asleep.

When the plane landed at Orlando International, the airport nearest the Kennedy Space Center, the passenger door swung open, and a blast of hot air whooshed through the cabin. The temperature that day was 103 degrees in the shade, one of the hottest days in Florida history. Mike refused to get into Carrie's backpack.

"We have to debark, Mikey," said Carrie.

"No way, Carrie. It's too hot. Tell the pilot to drive us over to Mission Control and keep the air-conditioning up high."

"Mike, you can't drive a 747 up route A1A," said Susan.

"A NASA pilot could," said Mike, who figured that if NASA could put men on the moon, they could drive a 747 up an interstate.

He remained in the seat looking like a wilted daisy and fanning with his hoof.

"NASA can do the launch right here. I can watch from the window," whined Mike, antlers drooping.

"You'd complain the window's too small, Mikey. Come on," said Carrie stretching out her arms to him.

The cab to the Space Center will be air conditioned," said Susan, clapping impatiently.

Mike, muttering about heat stroke, reluctantly let Carrie set him in her backpack. Passing through airport security he asked the guard for cold lemonade and salt pills. The guard heard nothing.

A VIP limo was holding for them out front.

"Hi, I'm Josh," said the driver. "Off to the Kennedy Space Center, right?" he said, after filling the trunk with their suitcases.

A tall man wearing cowboy boots and breathing heavily came running up.

"Josh," he said to their driver.

"Director Jones," said Josh, "Surprised to see you here at this hour, Sir. Especially on a launch day."

"Just got in. My flight was delayed. I should'a been at the center this morning. I assume you're headed there? Mind if I bum a ride? My driver is stuck in traffic."

Josh turned back to Susan. "Ma'am this is Director Jones, head of all of NASA. He needed to be at the Center hours ago. Would you mind if he rides with us since we're headed there?"

"Of course not," said Susan. "How do you do," she said reaching to shake his hand.

"Elroy Jones, Ma'am and Miss," said the director, tipping his tan Stetson twice.

"I'm Susan Grossman, and this is my daughter Carrie…and this…" but Susan didn't go further. She had second thoughts about introducing Mike.

"Pleased to meet you," said Director Jones, "and obliged for the lift. I should'a been at the Center hours ago."

"Kind of ironic, isn't it, Sir?" said Susan. "You're sending a ship to Mars but held up by a domestic flight."

"It is kind'a funny, isn't it," said Director Jones smiling.

Carrie noted that the director didn't dress like a typical executive. He wore a leather jacket, a cowboy hat and cowboy boots of tan and blue leather with silver-tipped toes.

Perched over Carrie's backpack, Mike eyed his boots and decided the silver boot tips were phony hoofs.

"Why are you pretending to have hooves?" Mike demanded. "Because I am not fooled, Mister. You needn't be ashamed of having human feet. They're not as good as hooves, but as Nurse Claire says, we have to accept our limitations and be who we are. You don't see me pretending by walking around in Nikes."

The director heard nothing, of course.

"Those are cowboy boots, Mike," Carrie whispered.

"About the handsomest I've ever seen," added Susan.

The director smiled at Susan's compliment although he noted that Carrie had his name wrong.

"Yup, Ms. Susan, you're looking at pure West African aborigine tanned ostrich leather sewn to native Blue Malaysian Coral snake skin from Australia. Mayor of Sidney gave 'em to me after our capsule landed off track in Lake Macquarie."

He settled back in his seat.

72

"I've read about you and the Mars Launch, Sir, and I saw your picture on the cover of *Time*," said Susan.

"Don't be fooled by his tin hooves, Mom. If he's a director, I'm a peacock,"

Carrie slid her hand over Mike's mouth, not that it mattered.

"The director is the Commander of all NASA operations. He headed the first moon expedition and is in charge of this Mars launch," said Josh, looking as proud as if he were the director's personal driver. "And Sir, the Grossmans are guests of the president."

"This launch'll be a thriller," said Director Jones.

Lowering his voice and leaning in as if to share a secret, he said in a half whisper, "First time we're deploying the new Cybertron Dentine Eco-Hybrid Co-Polarized rockets. Our new ones use magnetic thrusters powered by Hydrothermalated Co-Populated Ionized Polybarbitals," he said, assuming everyone knew about NASA's new fuel.

The other passenger's eyes looked glazed.

"It's the new fuel based solely on the principle of ultra-chemo-methane-thermo-hydrophonics."

Blank stares.

"You know - the chemical reaction you get when water and sub-nuclear fatty cholesterol molecules collide. Forty percent more power yet half the fuel weight."

"Of course," said Mike, who'd seen it on the *Discovery Channel*.

"That fuel is even more powerful than liquid hydrogen," said Carrie.

Director Jones nodded, pleased with her knowledge.

"So they pump it in the gas tank?" asked Susan, trying to be with it.

Director Jones shook his head.

"No ma'am," he said, as if helping a child tie a lace. "They insert fuel cells that stack like honeycombs."

"Ah huh," said Susan still clueless.

"Look Ma'am, a picture's better than words. Take my card," he said, handing Susan his business card. "Since you're guests of the president, if you'd like to come over a few hours before launch, say about four. Show my card at the gate. If time allows, I'll take you in the capsule, and you'll understand things better when you see them close up. I'll even introduce you to the crew while they're settling in."

On his card, the director wrote: "Susan and Carrie Grossman, my guests," and he signed it "EJ."

"What a wonderful opportunity, Sir," said Susan beaming.

The director's invitation seemed to change Mike the Moose's mind about him.

"Mike the Moose reporting, Director Jones, Sir," said Mike saluting with a hoof. "Ready for blast off. Induce trajectory – ah, make for the stars, dude. Carrie, this is so cool," said Mike.

Neither the director nor Josh heard Mike. But Carrie couldn't help sliding her hand gently over his mouth.

At the guardhouse, an alert young lieutenant, saw Director Jones and saluted. Josh sped the limo past the gate and stopped at the entrance to a massive, white complex of buildings that looked like a cross between a solar observatory and the Lincoln Memorial. The director thanked Susan and Carrie and nodded to Josh and departed.

Josh leaned over the seat. "After the third moon mission, President Kenyon awarded him the Medal of Honor for saving three men from sure death. He risked his life doing it. The director's a true American hero."

"A gentleman too," added Susan.

"Cool shoes," Mike said, now fully in favor of the director's silver-toed boots. "And while on the subject of heroes, Josh, did I show you my medal?"

Josh heard nothing.

Susan, and Carrie, with Mike in her backpack arrived at the gate just before four o'clock and presented the director's card.

"We are expecting you Ms. Grossman," said the guard, nodding.

At Mission Control they were led down corridors to an enormous room and directed to a row of chairs designated for VIP guests. The walls of the control room were filled with flashing monitors and blinking colored lights. Men and women wearing headsets and carrying clipboards moved quickly along the rows of consoles. Mike looked around the VIP area and saw several movie stars. Carrie noticed two Senators that she'd studied in current events class.

Mike, perched on the rim of Carrie's backpack, pointed to a nearby monitor. "What time is *The Simpsons*?" he asked.

"It's not that kind of screen, Mikey," said Susan.

"You mean they only get the dull stuff Dad watches – *Meet the Press* and *CNN*. BORING," said Mike. "Kids and mooselings pay taxes. We do, don't we, Mom? So wouldn't you think NASA could afford cable?"

"Those are mission monitors, Mikey, not TVs," explained Carrie. "They're for the Mars launch. That monitor," she pointed, "shows inside the space capsule. The engineers can see the astronauts thousands of miles out in space."

"Don't the astronauts want *The Simpsons?*" Mike asked.

"The monitors let them watch astronauts walking in space or making repairs to the capsule and doing aeronautical experiments. Space has no gravity so they float, weightless," Carrie explained.

"We should send Mom," giggled Mike. "She wants to lose weight. But the astronauts need TV. I read in *National Tabloid Weekly* that the human mind can only go four hours without TV before failing," he said with high authority.

Out of the corner of her eye, Susan noticed two security guards staring at her. They whispered and repeatedly turned back to Carrie and Susan.

"You're right," the first guard said to the other. "They're definitely speaking into the kid's backpack. We allow recording devices. So what are they hiding?"

"And if they are hiding something, what are they doing in a top security area?" said the other guard. "Check and see if the lady is a reporter."

The guard thumbed through his clipboard list of attending press.

"Nope, she's not on the press list. So why is she at NASA with a kid? Ah ha," he waved a second clipboard. "Says they are guests of the president and Director Jones."

"But what's that hanging out of the kid's backpack?" asked the guard.

They started towards Susan and Carrie, but Director Jones arrived and reached his guests first. The guards drew back.

"Howdy Susan, Ms. Carrie," said the director, tipping his hat. "Glad you made it. I'm about to board. Come have a look." He motioned that they follow.

"They must be okay if both the director and the president know them," said one guard to the other. "They are on the VIP list," he said, pointing to their names.

"But they're talking into that backpack," said the other guard shaking his head.

Carrie, Susan and the director trailed three fully-suited astronauts and approached the gleaming space craft. The astronauts moved heavily as if their boots were solid lead. Each step took them further up a heavy steel gangplank and closer to the great silver bird.

The cone's main door swiveled open, and an air lock released with a sharp hiss. Inside the capsule was a wall of dials, gauges, colored tubes, and blinking panels, as well as joysticks, keyboards and thruster throttles. Mike boosted himself slightly over the top of Carrie's backpack and had to rub his moose eyes to be sure it was real.

"Wow, Carrie," he said "This is better than our X-Box. A real space ship."

"Wow, Mike," Carrie agreed.

"Call me Earl," the director corrected Carrie, recalling that Susan had mistaken his name in the limo. "And yup, it is a 'WOW.' After all these years I can't get over it myself," he said reverently. "Come see what's beyond this portal." He led the way. "This is the centrifugal retrogressive sizematic chamber where astronauts shed suits and decompress before they enter the main cabin. And this porthole," he said, pointing to the largest window, "is where they egress and walk in space to make repairs. Those white suits they wear are a marvel. Regular little space ships themselves. They carry a two-hour oxygen supply and protect the astronauts from outside temperatures as cold as minus 240 Celsius."

"That's colder than the North Pole woods," thought Mike.

"And here's the communications center," said Director Jones, pointing to an array of speakers, throttles, buttons, and monitors. "Totally digital-co-axial with Bose surround sound and pentagonal transmission arrays – the works. Lets the crew talk to Mission Control thousands of miles away and sound like they're just next door."

"I can hear Dad complaining about the long distance bill," Mike whispered.

"For real," said Carrie.

"You bet it's for real," said Director Jones, assuming Carrie had asked a question. "Clear as if from the next room. It's amazing what we've accomplished with frequency modulation capitalization and double dip algorithms. Sounds in the range of human speech are isolated. They get magnified, while frequencies outside the human range are suppressed."

"Ah huh," said Susan, pretending again. "So...what do the astronauts eat?"

"Flavored soy cubes with nutritional supplements. Try a lobster," said Director Jones, tearing foil off a small red cube and handing it to her. She tossed it into her mouth.

"It actually tastes like lobster."

Director Jones opened a brown foil packet and placed a cube in Carrie's hand.

"It's chocolate cake," said Carrie, after a bite.

"Impressive, huh?" said the director.

"Boring!" Mike complained. "How about a McDouble Burger with Biggie Fries, a Super-Size shake...and, ah, a slice of pepperoni pizza?"

"How are you going to get pizza in outer space?" muttered Carrie.

"Ah, sorry, little lady," said the director overhearing, "we don't have pizza cubes. But we do have Neapolitan ice cream." Director Jones pointed to a pink, brown and white tricolored foil.

"A dopey desert," said Mike, poking his antlers over Carrie's backpack. The director noticed Mike for the first time and stopped.

"What's that?" he asked.

"Duh," huffed Mike the Moose annoyed.

Carrie struggled to push Mike down her pack, but it was too late. Mike had pushed his way up again.

Carrie had to say something. "Ah... Ah... I have a little, ah... mooseling."

"A gift for someone?"

"Not exactly," Susan interrupted.

"Cute," said Director Jones, tweaking Mike's nose.

"Cute?" said Mike the Moose. "Cute? You hyper-inflated astro-blob. You, Sir are talking to the most highly decorated moose ever. Why I could pick up that phone," said Mike gesturing to a handset on the capsule wall, "and call the President of the United States. He said I could anytime. Didn't he, Mom? Bet *you* can't get him on the phone, Mr. Phony Hooves."

The director heard nothing, but Susan said, "Mike, hush. Please."

That's when it dawned on Director Jones that Susan was talking to a toy moose atop Carrie's backpack. He suddenly had second thoughts about the guests he invited aboard a highly secret spacecraft.

"It was a mistake," he thought, "to invite them on the capsule without checking them out thoroughly. But didn't Josh say they were guests of the president?"

Desperate to change the subject, Susan asked, "How do they keep air in here?"

"Well Susan," said Director Jones, ignoring her question and gently taking her arm, "it's time to debark." He beckoned Carrie to follow. "Only fifty-five minutes 'till lift. This way please," he said, rushing them down the plank as politely but as fast as he could.

Carrie turned to follow at just the wrong time and bumped head on into the First Officer astronaut who was coming through the air lock. She practically bounced off of his inflated suit. The silver face-guard on the officer's helmet lowered electrically.

"Sorry, young lady," he said. "You okay?"

"My fault totally," Carrie apologized.

Director Jones hurried them down the gangplank just as the third astronaut entered the capsule, and, with another loud hiss, the massive door lock rotated shut.

"Hurry, please," prodded Director Jones.

Susan noticed the director now spoke to her slowly, as if to a child.

"Come Susan and Carrie, and I'll take you for a nice view of lift-off," he said, forcing a smile.

Watching lift-off through mission control's foot thick windows was like seeing the world from inside a furnace. Carrie couldn't take her eyes off the thundering tunnels of fire that flared off the capsule's tail. It was better than the launches she'd seen on TV, and she felt the power as the NASA building shook. Rockets bigger than school buses inched off the pad, slowly at first, then faster, faster until they jumped like stones from a sling shot.

"Unbelievable, huh Mikey," said Carrie, looking skyward.

Mike said nothing.

"First time I've ever found you speechless, Mikey," said Carrie.

She peeked into her backpack to see Mike's expression.

No Mike.

Carrie dug into her backpack. No Mike.

"Mom, he's not here," said Carrie.

"Of course he is, Carrie," said Susan.

Carrie slid her backpack to her front and searched frantically.

"Mom, he isn't," cried Carrie panicking. "Oh, Mom," she said. "You don't suppose I dropped Mike on the launch pad?" A terrible vision of 1000-degree flames engulfing her mooseling brother turned Carrie's face ash-white.

"The little guy would be gone in a second," Susan whispered, growing more worried.

They turned to retrace their steps, walking down the hallway toward the gangplank searching for Mike. The two security guards hurried after them.

Back on the capsule, Mike opened his eyes and rubbed a bump on his forehead.

Then it came back to him. "Carrie collided with the First Officer and I was knocked from her backpack," Mike remembered. "I went antlers first, cartwheeling to the floor, and hit my head on the hard steel. I must have gone unconscious."

Mike arose on wobbly front hooves and shook his fur.

Vim-BAM-bam-bam-bam.

He heard the loud sound. The capsule had jettisoned its auxiliary fuel tanks. Mike recalled seeing the process on the *Discovery Channel,* and through the porthole he watched the big tank tumble end over end towards Earth. Then silence as the ship slipped through dark endless space. In the forward command console, Mike watched the crew of three remove their safety harnesses and slowly get up from their seats. Andy Nielson, the first officer, noticed Mike first.

"What in the universe is this?" said Andy, approaching and lifting Mike off the floor and squeezing him like a fish.

"Oww. Don't squeeze me so hard you galactic-goofus," hollered Mike at the top of his lungs. "I'm not toothpaste!"

First Officer's Nielson's mouth dropped. He shook his head and rubbed his eyes.

"What on Earth...?"

"You poor dude; you are as lost as you look." said Mike. "This is outer space not Earth." Mike pointed out the porthole at the darkness and spoke to the first officer the way a professor might teach a D-student. But Mike was surprised too. It seemed the first officer heard him.

The captain and the navigator gathered around Mike.

"How'd they get it to speak?" asked the captain.

"I wonder if it's because we are in outer space that they can hear me," Mike wondered aloud. "Or maybe it has something to do with the lack of gravity?"

"Holy Neptune y'all," First Officer Nielsen said again, holding up Mike. "It spoke. More than that. Somehow it's responding to what I say. This is more than a play-back machine. I'll bet the guys at Center are controlling it remotely."

Mike waved a hoof.

"Holy Neptune y'all. It talks," said Mike, perfectly mimicking the First Office's southern accent.

Captain Scott Bradford and Navigator Judy Barnes looked at each other. Captain Bradford started laughing and Judy did too.

"You are right, little moose. Our First Officer does speak… although for a long time we weren't sure if that southern drawl was English."

The captain winked at Judy. First Officer Nielsen looked annoyed.

"Let me have a look," said Captain Bradford, reaching for Mike.

Baffled, First Officer Nielsen handed Mike over.

"Hi, Sir," said Mike smiling. "Mike the Moose, Master of Marbles at your service." He offered a hoof salute.

"So you talk?" marveled the captain. "Your robotics must be amazing," he muttered.

The captain leaned into his console microphone.

"This your little surprise, Director Jones?"

The console speakers were silent.

"Okay, Mission Control," said Captain Bradford, "You put a good one over on us this time."

Captain Bradford stared at the monitors, expecting the Mission Control team to burst into laughter. Silence.

Mike was annoyed.

"Look, you sub-atomic particle. Did you call me a robot? You speak, and I don't call you one," said Mike

The captain did a mock apologetic bow.

"I am most sorry, Your Antlership," said Captain Bradford.

The captain looked at his monitor; the Mission Control team appeared, wide-eyed and silent.

Though growing impatient with the joke, Captain Bradford decided to continue playing along.

"So Mike may I ask how you boarded a top security space capsule?" Mike shrugged.

Captain Bradford turned to First Officer Nielsen and whispered, "You don't think Mission Control is springing a psyche evaluation? Usually I get a heads up when one's coming."

The first officer looked bewildered.

Captain Bradford pushed a button on his console.

"Okay Control, what's the story? Control? Hello. Mission Control?"

Finally a voice boomed through Captain Bradford's speaker.

"We hear you, Bradford. VoiceCom was out for a moment." Director Jones himself appeared in the monitor holding a microphone.

"You can let me in on your little moose joke now," said Captain Bradford, smiling.

There wasn't a giggle from the speaker. After a long pause, Director Jones came back, but his voiced lacked its authority.

"Say again, Bradford?"

"Moose. Your little moose joke. What's with the moose?" said Captain Bradford impatiently.

"What's loose?" asked Director Jones. "We're monitoring that all systems are normal. Don't tell me the carbonic digestive regenerator went bad again, did it, Bradford?"

"Not l-o-o-s-e. Moose. M-O-O-S-E," said Captain Bradford holding Mike up to the video eye.

Back on Earth, Mike's snout alone appeared on thirty monitors all at once. Then, as Captain Bradford held him further back, Mike's eyes appeared, then his antlers, and finally, all of Mike the Moose showed on the Center's screens.

"Holy sagebrush," said Director Jones.

"Oh, thank goodness. It's my brother," said Carrie, jumping from her chair and pointing to the monitor. "He's safe, Mom." Carrie's voice was filled with relief.

"Good lord, it's their stuffed toy," said Director Jones, eying Susan suspiciously. The two security guards moved in to flank Susan and Carrie. Mission Control buzzed as everyone tried to figure out what was going on.

"How did that toy get on board?" Director Jones demanded of Susan.

Staff whispers turned to gasps when from thousands of miles out in space Mike's voice boomed back.

"Do you think I want to be here? It's not like I saved up for a ticket," huffed Mike the Moose.

"It's responsive too," said the director. "Acts like it has intelligence."

"Wish I could say the same of you, Director Phony Hooves. Who forgot to insert your Coppertops? Open your pad and take a note. Of course I'm intelligent. I have one of the highest Moose MENSA IQs ever recorded. I'm the intelligence you've been hunting for in outer space. I don't want to be here but I am...me...Mike the Moose, Master of Marbles."

There was a long, stunned pause before Director Jones broke the silence.

"Bradford, if you know anything about this, now would be a good time to drop the foolishness."

"Are you saying this isn't your idea?" Captain Bradford's voice came back. "Does anyone know about this?" said Bradford, turning to his two crew members.

Blank looks.

"Okay, listen up," said the director, "control staff, and you on the capsule. Y'all get this, and get it pronto. I don't know what's happening here, but effective immediately, 0-1800 hours," Director Jones eyed the digital clock on his monitor, "I'm imposing priority-one mission silence. I want no press, no calls home – none to associates or vendors. I want total and I mean one hundred percent silence until we figure this out. Break this silence – you're gone for good."

The capsule crew and control staff nodded like summer camp kids.

"Security," continued the director, "find what in the galaxy that thing on board is and how it got there. Go to Threat Level One 'til we know more."

"Yo. Mr. Director." Mike's voice came through the console speaker. "Got anything to eat up here? Usually Carrie makes me lunch by 0-1200 hours. I like pizza. Or a burger, medium rare – hold the onions, please. Hate onions. I like chocolate...a shake?"

The director's mouth could have caught flies. He turned to Susan and Carrie. His security guards moved in closer as the director peppered Susan with questions.

"Who do you work for? What is that moose thing really, and how'd the two of you manage to plant it on the capsule? We have ways of finding out, you know."

Director Jones nodded to a member of his team and computers spun through a database of suspects and used face-recognition software to search for Susan or Carrie's true identities.

"Whoa," said Susan. "One question at a time. We're guests, not spies."

"Sir. I think Mikey may have fallen from my backpack. Remember, Director Jones, when I bumped into the captain – when you led us from the capsule," Carrie offered. "But Sir, Mike's just a little mooseling. He's my brother, Mr. Director. He's no threat. He helped the State Department once."

Director Jones shook his head.

"It's true and we can prove it," Susan said. "We're guests. Call this man at State Department headquarters. He's the head of their agents." She reached into her purse and thumbed for Agent Harry Malone's card. "It was just an accident. We want our moose back safe. He's no threat. He's a little mooseling, for goodness sake."

"Sure, lady," said one of the security guards. "Nothing unusual about a stowaway talking moose on a NASA space ship bound for Mars."

"It's odd that you can all hear him, though. We always can," Susan explained. "And some kids can. But few adults can and when they do, we never know why. The President of the United States hears him," Susan said matter-of-factly.

Director Jones rolled his eyes, embarrassed that it was he who had invited the crazy woman on the capsule.

"I think there's something about being in space that explains it, Mom," said Carrie, ignoring the director's suspicious look. "Maybe it's the lack of gravity? Or the artificial gravity? Or the oxygen levels?"

Director Jones, recovered slightly from the shock, barked orders. "Captain Bradford," he bellowed into his microphone, "take that toy…"

Mike's annoyed face appeared in the monitor. "Look dude…" He was about to let the director have it when Susan cut him short.

"Skip the tirade, Mike," said Susan. "The director was just surprised, that's all."

"He wasn't trying to be mean," added Carrie.

"That's right, I'm not being mean," said Director Jones addressing Mike directly for the first time. "So Bradford, you get that toy and..."

Mike scowled.

"I mean...Bradford...you take the nice moose," said Director Jones in a placating voice.

Mike's toothy smile appeared in the monitors.

"Ah...take, ah, MIKE to the sterile room and check it, ah HIM for contaminates. If he's clean, get back on schedule but watch him. The mission's already an hour behind and we're losing valuable time. But Bradford, this is NOT something I planned. Frankly, I don't know what it is. But get the mission back on track until we know more. That is AFTER you are 100 percent sure that it's, ah, that he's clean."

"Clean?" Mike's voice came back. "Look Director MoonWalk, I'm not some kind of space urchin. I brush my teeth three times daily, moving my toothbrush up and down like mom taught me." Gleaming moose teeth appeared on 100 mission monitors at once.

"And I wash with soap and water before breakfast, lunch and dinner. By the way, where is lunch? I wash my face and hooves at bedtime before prayers. Ask Mom if I don't. Mom tell 'em...," said Mike as Captain Bradford pulled him away from the camera.

"Take Mike to the sterile room, straight away, please," Captain Bradford said to Judy.

"Hey, tell 'em about the fresh T-shirt Carrie put on me before we left..." said Mike protesting in the background as Navigator Judy Barnes carried him away.

Director Jones and the guards led Susan and Carrie to an interrogation room.

"I'm just a mother," said Susan from her chair.

He's my mooseling brother," Carrie insisted.

"Ya'll get the CIA file back on those two yet?" barked the director to his guards.

The first security guard left to check on it. The second security guard clicked on a hanging light that hurt Susan's eyes.

Back on the space capsule, Mike entertained the fascinated crew.

"So you see," Mike explained, "with my knowledge of moon craters I'm perfect to lead a landing party. Once and for all we can get to the bottom of the cheese rumor."

"We're headed for Mars, not the moon, and there's no cheese on either planet, my little friend," said an amused Captain Bradford. "And we don't have a space suit quite your size."

"But that's the beauty of it," said Mike excitedly. "I don't need a space suit or oxygen like you guys do. I can look into small crevices. You can't. We could make history together," said Mike, geared up. "One small step for man, a hoof print for moosekind," he said, hooves waving.

The crew quickly warmed to Mike.

Mike presented his theory of why Mars was red.

"Under the lava is the Sea of Red Jaw Breakers," said Mike. "It's gigantic..."

Then it happened.

A huge BLAMMmmm rocked the capsule followed by the sound of shearing metal.

The capsule lurched sideways, then rolled. Red console lights flashed and gauge needles wavered like windshield wipers. A mechanical computer voice repeated, "Threat Level Four. Threat Level Four."

Captain Bradford scanned his instruments.

"We're hit, Mission Control. Space debris or a small meteor. It perforated the cone. I see a quarter inch hole in the dorsal dentrical exterior shield," said the captain, zooming the monitor in on a large hole in the hull.

No one including Mike was joking now.

Director Jones' voice boomed, "Is it as bad as it looks, Bradford?"

"'fraid so," said Captain Bradford. "Whatever perforated the right tile on the cogenerative protractor valve – well, we're retaining air pressure for the moment – but we won't on reentry."

"Looks like only the thin shell's left in place," said Director Jones. "Reentry will blow it apart for sure. No choice but to abort the mission. We'll burn the reverse thrusters and get you headed back. We'll need some time for the computers to plot your new course. But I don't know how we'll deal with reentry"

"Roger," said Captain Bradford.

"Not cool," muttered Mike. "How'd I get up here anyway? I want to go home and be with Carrie. Right now."

7

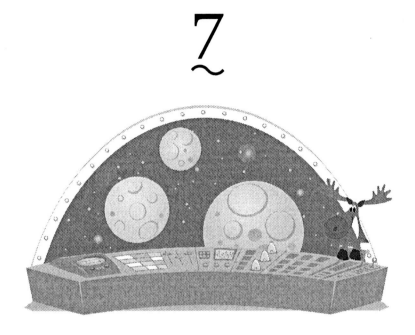

MIKE AND THE SPACE SHIP

For another twenty minutes the wounded craft bore them deeper into space until finally Director Jones' voice boomed again.

"Bradford."

"Sir?"

Standby please. At 0-1448 initiate the dentrical thrusters. We're bringing ya home Son."

"Roger," said Captain Bradford.

"Make it so," said Mike the Moose, imitating Star Trek's Captain Picard and giving the captain a hoof bump. Mike approached a console microphone. "Please tell Mom and Carrie I'm ready to come home. And to hurry."

He floated back to Captain Bradford's lap where the Captain buckled Mike in with him, stroking his antlers. "Don't worry, little guy," he said. "We'll get you back."

Mike felt calmed by his words. He liked Captain Bradford.

"Start the blast countdown," came a Mission Control voice.

"10-9-8-7…"

Mike trembled at each number.

"It's okay, Mike," reassured Captain Bradford.

"...6-5-4-3-2-"

Mike was shaking.

"1."

A huge blast came from the rear of the capsule and the cabin lights dimmed. Mike felt the capsule roll and was pushed back into the Captain's tummy. Mike's chest felt like there was a refrigerator on it. The ship accelerated, shuddering under the power of blasting thrusters, and it performed a successful course reversal.

"I...I...I...I waaa nnaaa ggooo hoomme," said Mike, having a hard time with the G-force.

Captain Bradford stroked Mike until the heaviness lifted. Then all was dark as the tiny capsule hurled silently towards Earth at thousands of miles an hour.

When the lights resumed, the peaceful silence of deep space was quickly broken by Mike the Moose who slid from under the Captain's seat belt and stood on the console.

"So," said Mike, as if he'd never stopped talking, "I've got this space thing down pat. Not to worry. I'll navigate us back just like I saw Homer Simpson do on TV. It's not so hard."

From her seat, Navigator Judy Barnes burst out laughing. The comic relief was exactly what the crew needed. Even the Mission Control crew, monitoring the imperiled craft, started smiling. Mike moonwalked at the throttles, and laughter broke out in the capsule in space and the control center on Earth.

"Well I can so handle the navigation," said Mike, not sure how to take the laughter.

All too soon the tension built again as the ship neared reentry. When the capsule entered the outer rings of Earth's atmosphere, the crew felt a sudden shudder. Then came the sound everyone feared – the shriek of tearing metal – so awful that Mike covered his ears. Both teams – on Earth and in the fragile capsule – froze as if somebody hit 'pause' with a TV remote.

Glued to his monitor Captain Bradford was first to see the long fracture appear in the cone's metal surface. It looked like a paper tear, but deeper.

"Sisssss." They heard capsule's precious oxygen slowly leaking into space.

"Center," Captain Bradford's voice was high-pitched, "we've lost our seal. That's it." The captain looked at his watch. "We've got an hour of flight but only a half hour of oxygen in our suit tanks. Crew set your masks to sleep mode immediately," he ordered.

The astronauts quickly slipped into their space suits and adjusted the flow to minimize oxygen consumption.

"We're on our tanks, Center," said Bradford lowering his voice, "but there isn't enough. To make matters worse, AutoNav is dead, and the backup system is blinking red too."

The CIA report came back on Susan and Carrie. Agent Malone vouched for them and confirmed they were legitimate guests of the president. But the director cut Malone short when he started to vouch for Mike the Moose too. Director Jones made a mental note that when the crisis was over he would request a copy of Malone's psychiatric profile. After a nod from the director, the security guards led Susan and Carrie back to their VIP seats.

Carrie repeatedly gripped her chair arms, waiting for word about Mike. Susan paced at the window nearby.

"A water landing is best," said Director Jones. "When the crew goes unconscious at least we can deploy the parachute remotely. That's still working. I'm worried about the throttles as much as anything. The oxygen-starved crew won't be conscious to operate them."

The engineers nodded in anxious agreement.

Back on the capsule the air tank gauges on the crew suits dipped into the red. Precious little oxygen remained as they entered the second layer of Earth's atmosphere. The craft's tiny exterior, a delicate eggshell in vast dark space, glowed orange from the intense heat.

Mike floated over to the captain's console, starting up again about his navigating skills, when he noticed that both Captain Bradford and First Officer Nielsen had nodded off. Mike saw their oxygen-starved bloodshot eyes.

"Geez, I'm not that boring," said Mike looking worried. "At-ten-hup," he yelled.

Captain Bradford's eyes blinked half open. He starred at Mike but his look was dull.

Mike tried to stir him, "Are you taking me home or not!"

Captain Bradford seemed to comprehend but groggily responded, "Too littttle air."

In slow motion the captain forced his arm towards the console. He tapped the glass on the oxygen gauge, hoping against hope it would jump from the red zone. The needle held fast.

"Bradford. Bradford," boomed the console speaker. "Oxygen critical. Do you copy? Can you hang on ten more minutes for throttle up? Bradford? Copy center? Bradfrord?"

"Ssscenterr," muttered Captain Bradford. His word came out like water over rocks, trailing away as his head snapped down and his eyes closed. Mike saw him try to lift his head with all his might; he couldn't. Captain Bradford, the last to pass out, had joined the First Officer and Navigator Judy Barnes in a dangerous oxygen-deprived, deep sleep.

"They've lost consciousness," said Director Jones and the AutoNav is fried."

Mike heard panic in Director Jones' voice.

"We can reposition the capsule and land by remote," Director Jones said to his staff, "but with the AutoNav dead only the crew can throttle the retro rockets. And nobody's conscious to do it."

Simultaneously, the control monitors turned brown as Mike the Moose stuck his snout in the camera.

"I can do it."

"Thank the heavens one of them is still conscious!" said Director Jones.

Mike's antlers were so close to the speaker that Director Jones' booming voice nearly blew his hooves out from under him.

"Easy on the decibels, Your Directorness," Mike complained, rubbing his antlers.

Mike moved back for a better camera position and appeared in full on a triple row of mission monitors.

"Great galaxy, it's the toy," said Director Jones.

Carrie rolled her eyes, knowing what was coming.

"Noooooo wayyyyyy, Noooooo toooy, Director ToadBuster." Mike's voice sounded from all the speakers at once. "I'm no toy, and I'm also not deaf, so lower your voice to preserve my antlers. It is not acceptable that you risk the precious hearing of a moose, and I want a written apology on NASA letterhead. FedEx it to me, and say that you're sorry," said Mike folding his moose arms.

Susan jumped from her seat and took the microphone out of the stunned director's hand.

"Listen up, Mike. I want zero attitude from you."

There was a pause and a crackle before Mike replied.

"Mom. Mom. Wow am I glad it's you. These guys are all sleeping." Mike's voice lowered, and his chest slumped. "And I don't think they're supposed to be sleeping. I want to come home. Now, please. What do I do?"

"It's okay, Mike. Yes, the crew is in trouble. You're speeding to Earth, and you're the only one left awake up there. But you can help Mike. So could you please, please do everything the nice Mission Control Director says," said Susan, handing the microphone back to the grateful director.

"I think he can help you, Sir," said Susan.

After a brief delay Mike saw Director Jones' face appear in the monitor.

"Mike, this is Director Jones. Can you hear me?"

"I can help, Your Directorness," said Mike again backing away from the microphone. "But easy on my ears please."

"Mike, you may be our last hope. You really think you can help?"

After a pause, the director's words sunk in. "Last hope, huh," said Mike. "I like that." Mike's antlers grew nearly an inch as he drew himself up.

"I hear you loud and clear, Sir. It's I, Mike the Moose, Master of Marbles, the much-decorated mooseling at your service. On this historic flight I stand ready…" Mike put his hoof over his heart, "…to come to the aid of my country and…"

"NOT NOW, MIKE," Carrie's voice interrupted.

"Mike, you're hurtling at a thousand miles an hour. Last hope remember. DANGER. Got that, Mike?" said Susan, almost as annoyed as anxious.

"Geez, Mom," muttered Mike.

Captain Bradford opened an eye and tried his best to say something, but he couldn't. He fell unconscious again.

"Mike," said Director Jones. "Do you think you can budge one of those throttles on the console?

"Well…" said Mike.

"I need you to pull it all the way forward. Then wait. Then, when I tell you to, push it back again? Do you have the strength?"

"But you jest." Mike flexed his leg, revealing the tiniest hint of moose muscle. "Who do you think Schwarzenegger wanted for his personal trainer. Who taught Popeye about spinach. I…"

"MIKE!" Susan cut him off.

"Geez, Mom," said Mike, dropping the flex.

"Great, Mike," said the director. "Do you see three throttles on the console ahead? There on your left? One's red, one's black and one's green – three handles?"

Mike looked.

"One, two, three…yes, Sir Director Jones," reported Mike.

"And you see that the one in the middle is black?" asked Director Jones.

"I see it. I see it," said Mike, getting excited.

"When I tell you can you, pull it towards yourself – full forward towards the window? Are you sure you can?" The director sounded worried.

"No problem-O, Your Directorship. Piece of cake, Dude," said Mike. Then, after a moment's pause, "Carrie I can, can't I?" asked Mike, sounding unsure.

"You absolutely can, Mike," Carrie's voice came back. "But do exactly what the director says."

"'K, Carrie," said Mike, feeling confident again.

"Good. Get in front of the throttle and wait until I tell you. When I say 'go'…pull it forward. Then wait a bit until I tell you to do it again – but this time push it back in the other direction."

"K," said Mike.

"Stand at the black throttle now. Yes, that's it. Now when I tell you, pull forward."

"Copy loud and clear. Over and out …Roger Dodger…"

"MIKE!" Carrie's hollered.

"Okay," said Mike.

"Ten seconds now, Mike," said Director Jones, eying the second hand on the console clock. "Put your hooves on the black throttle Mike. Yes, good. That's it. Get a strong footing."

"'K, Mr. Director," said Mike nervously.

Mike braced his hooves and leaned towards the black throttle awaiting the director's command.

"NOW MIKE!" said Director Jones. "Pull."

Mike pulled forward on the throttle with all the strength in his little mooseling body. Nothing happened.

Director Jones turned pale.

"Try again," urged Carrie.

Mike pulled again. This time, slowly, almost imperceptibly at first, the throttle edged slightly forward, then further forward until Mike had it pulled into full thrust position. The huge roar of the rear thrusters rattled the space capsule. Tremendous applause and cheering burst through the console from the Mission Control engineers.

"Mike, Mike. Mike. Go Mike," cheered the engineers.

Mike, forgetting there was more to, do began moonwalking the console adding hip flips.

"MIKE," screamed Carrie. "Get to that black throttle. DO IT NOW. Be ready to push it back when you are told."

"You're not done," Susan hollered.

"4-5-6-7," said Director Jones in the middle of the second count-up.

Mike rushed to the black throttle and put his back into it and was ready to push in the opposite direction. Director Jones continued the count.

"8-9…Get ready, Mike."

"Be ready, Mikey," Susan echoed.

"You can do it," said Carrie.

"10. PUSH IT BACK NOW, MIKE," shouted Director Jones.

Mike pushed with all his strength. Again the throttle didn't move. The ship was heading to Earth at a cataclysmic speed.

"Dig your hooves in," said Director Jones.

Mike dug in and gave the throttle the last bit he had left. Finally it moved, rotating back, back, back.

"A little more, Mike," pleaded Director Jones.

In the background Mike heard the mission staff urging, "Come on Mike."

Mike mustered his last bit of energy and pushed as hard as he could. His legs slid and he slipped to the floor, but miraculously the throttle came to rest in the full-off position.

"Helluva Texas-sized push, Mike!" said Director Jones.

The Mission Control engineers jumped to their feet, high-five bumping with their clip boards.

Mike remained exhausted at the base of the throttle, too tired to talk – one of the rare times in the young mooseling's history that ever occurred. His silence lasted almost a whole minute before he dragged himself up, and though slowly, dancing a football player's end zone shuffle.

"Mike. Hey Mike," said Director Jones. "One more thing, Mike."

Mike could barely hear the director above the cheering.

"MIKE." Carrie got his attention.

"Can you also hit that green button to the left of the throttle?" asked the director pointing left.

Mike put his hoof over a green button.

"That's the one, Mike," said Director Jones. "That'll release the pressure lock, and since we are back in atmosphere, the crew will get oxygen faster."

"Easy-Breezy, Director," said Mike, hopping on the green button. A loud hiss sounded as the air lock released, and Earth's oxygen flowed quickly into the capsule.

The tiny craft floated gently through the atmosphere as its parachute deployed.

"You're my man, Mike the Moose," said Director Jones.

Mike starred at him.

"I mean my moose," Director Jones corrected.

The cheering from Center was feverish. Mike took a bow, and figuring this was as good a time as ever, started to deliver the speech he'd given a hundred times since getting his medal from Spain.

"My fellow Americans," he brought his face to the microphone. "In this historic moment of moose greatness…"

Mercifully, no one at Mission Center had to listen. They saw Mike mouthing words, but they came without sound. A lady engineer who read lips burst out laughing. But the capsule was fully back in Earth's atmosphere and gravity had again taken hold. Whatever condition had allowed them to hear Mike was over as the small craft drifted down to the sea.

The crew of three stirred as if from a long winter nap. Captain Bradford shook his head.

"What happened?" He turned to Judy. "How'd you manage the safe reentry? Great job throttling down."

"Wasn't me." Judy shrugged. "I thought you did it," she said looking around the capsule as much in the dark about it as Captain Bradford.

"Must have been Andy?"

"Wazzn't me," slurred the First Officer, his eyes opening slowly.

"Good job, Bradford," said Director Jones through the console. "Splash down in 2 minutes and 22 seconds. The Navy has two ships heading to intercept. And on a personal note, your families are here awaiting our heroes."

Captain Bradford was pleased but befuddled. He noticed Mike on the console and smiled, remembering his little friend. "Hi, little guy. Glad to see you're okay. Let me strap you in with me for splash down."

Mike smiled too. "Nice guy," he thought. "He can come on my space missions anytime. It's been a good day, but enough is enough, even for a moosling," Mike decided.

"I just want my family," he said as Captain Bradford secured him gently under his shoulder harness. "Space is cool but mooselings have a preference for terra firma."

Captain Bradford didn't hear a word.

Back at Mission Control, a team of engineers debriefed the crew and Mike too. Carrie acted as Mike's voice. When the debriefing finished, Director Jones asked Susan, Carrie, and Captain Bradford to remain. Having been fully informed of Mike's bravery, Captain Bradford asked if he might hold the little mooseling in his lap.

Director Jones spoke.

"If the public ever found out that it took Mike to save us from a terrible disaster, congress would cut our funding like that," he said snapping his thumb. The captain's head nodded like a dashboard bobble toy.

"So for that and for security reasons none of you may say a word about this," the director explained. "No one would believe it anyway."

"Got that right," echoed Captain Bradford shaking his head.

"But," Susan added, "NASA knows how special you are Mike, and they hold you in their highest regard."

Mike rolled his eyes, "Bummer, Mom. So I save the mission and they want to keep it a secret? I could'a made the *Tonight Show*."

Mike paused a moment, thinking. "Can't I at least tell Agent Malone? Oggie? Boris?"

"Nope," said Carrie.

"My friend, Mr. President?"

"Actually, he knows all about it, Mike. But he, too, asks that you keep your role a secret. Can you do that?"

"Geezzzzz, Carrie," said Mike.

"I know Mike, but country first, remember?" Susan reminded.

"K, Mom," said Mike, but his antlers drooped.

"But we really appreciate what you did, Mike," said Director Jones.

"Well okay. You can count on me," said Mike. "But for my next mission, no food cubes. I want real pizza – lots of pepperoni and hold the onions please. Deal?"

They flew home in NASA's private jet, and Carrie held Mike in her lap. For the whole ride north, Mike couldn't stop talking about space.

"This private jet is no big deal, Carrie," Mike explained. "Domestic flights just can't compare."

A stewardess leaned across and set a plate on Carrie's tray. On the plate was a full-sized 14" sizzling pizza – pepperoni – hold the onions. Next to the plate was a note:

"Mike, I hope the food on this leg of your trip is more to your liking. Thank you again, my brave friend."

The note was signed, *EJ*.

The Grossman family was together again in the living room. Stephen had finished his work assignment. Mike and Carrie played marbles near the warmth of logs aglow in the fireplace. Eddie, Kola and Cooper lay curled on their dog beds. Susan knitted and Stephen turned on the TV for an afternoon of football.

"I could never play football, Carrie," said Mike.

"Why not?"

"Do they make helmets with antler holes?"

"I see what you mean," said Carrie.

The doorbell rang. Stephen opened it and found a UPS package at the front door. Stephen read the label.

"It's addressed to a Mr. Mike the Moose, Master of Marbles. Anyone here by that name?" he asked.

"Very funny, Dad," said Mike stretching for the package.

"There's a letter inside. Want me to read it to you, Mike?" Stephen offered.

"Please, Dad."

"It's printed on White House stationary."

"Oh, hurry, Dad," said Mike.

"Okay," said Stephen. "It reads:

```
Dear Mike the Moose;

Director Jones and Agent Malone told me all
about your unexpected adventure. You are
indeed the most special moose ever, aren't
you."
```

Mike waved his hooves. "I am. I am, aren't I, Dad."

"Would you like me to continue?" Stephen asked.

"Sorry, Dad. Yes, keep reading," said Mike.

```
"And so, Mike, while I regret that I can't
tell the world how heroic a moose you are,
I want you to know that your country and
I are so proud of you. Your bravery is an
example for all living creatures.

While I can't thank you publicly, my little
friend, I have something special I think
you may like.
```

Stephen peeked inside the box.

"What is it, Dad? What?" asked Mike.

Stephen continued:

```
"You probably know, Mike, that before we
attempted the manned Mars Mission you were
on, we made an unmanned Mars Mission voyage
- a robotic trial trip that did make it the
entire way to Mars and back. Our spacecraft
returned to Earth with samples of Martian
soil."
```

Mike's antlers dropped. "Carrie," he muttered, "don't tell me my special gift is space dirt."

Stephen lifted a small leather pouch from the box, took something from it, and held up a tiny gleaming blue orb that glowed like a bulb. Stephen read on.

> "To the surprise of the scientists, Mike, one of the pieces of Mars matter is shaped like a perfect globe. It's just amazing, and it shines brilliantly - like gold, but it has a blue halo. We've never seen anything like it.
>
> It's perfectly safe to touch and, in fact, Mr. Mike the Moose, some of us are of the opinion that this special Mars stone looks very much like a...

"...MARBLE!" Mike interrupted excitedly as Stephen handed him the gleaming orb, before reading more of the president's words.

> "It's priceless, Mike, and I promise you there is nothing like it on Earth. Maybe not in the whole solar system.
>
> So Mike, your nation salutes you. You, Mike the Moose, Master of Marbles, are the bravest moose I've ever known (even if I know only one.)
>
> Please stay in touch, my heroic friend,
> *Edward Casterbridge Kenyon, III*
> President of the United States of America"

The blue glow from Mike's marble lit the room.

"Wow, WOw WOW," said Mike the Moose, Master of Marbles as he admired his best marble ever. "It's so totally galactic, Carrie. I really like it, don't you? I should thank the president a ton. And I need to get a message to Director Jones, too," said Mike. "Tell him if he needs me for the next launch, I'm in. Although I'd prefer to know in advance."

As Mike neared the edge of sleep that night he thought, "my life has changed so much since the day Carrie rescued me from the yard sale. I wanted a family of my own – a big sister, and a mom and a dad – a real home. (Though one without crockigators, of course.) I even like Eddie, Cooper and Kola, despite that they're dogs. And I still have my best friends – Boris and Humpy.

"I am one happy mooseling," Mike decided.

I was worried I wouldn't fit in, in a human family. After all, moose and men have their differences. I feel sorry for some things about humans. Some men go bald. We moose never do. And imagine having feet instead of hooves. No wonder Director Jones wears fake silver ones. But he turned out to be a pretty neat guy. (I especially liked him after he sent the piz-za-with-pepperoni-hold-the-onions on my plane trip home.)

But the biggest difference of all is that I've never seen a man, not even Dad, with a proud rack of antlers. Humans have limitations.

"I love my family," thought Mike. "And although we're not exactly the same, I fit in perfectly. I wouldn't admit it out loud," thought Mike, "but I love Carrie even more than marbles. Well...okay, she's tied with my Mars marble. But she's more fun to play with. My sister's really, really nice."

Mike peeked over at Carrie, smiled, closed his eyes, and drifted off to his most beautiful dream ever. He was in this space capsule heading for a planet made entirely of strawberry's when suddenly...

Mike's dream continued wherever mooslings dream...a place revealed to humans only if Mike tells us when he wakes.

About the Author

I Michael Grossman's other books include his first, *Coming to Terms with Aging, the Secret to Meaningful Time*, his memoir, *Shrinkwrapped: My First Fifty Years on the Couch*—originally published by RDR Books and now by the EBook Bakery, and *The Power*, Grossman's first fiction.

Writings include newspaper articles, commentaries, consumer and trade articles on wide-ranging topics ranging from ecology, ethics, travel marketing, bank marketing, flying, and applied ergonomics. His articles have appeared in *Advertising Age, Ergo Solutions, The CLIA Cruise Industry Annual Report, The American Banker* and *Plane and Pilot*. Grossman has appeared on national radio and TV shows including Arthur Frommer's Travel Channel show and NBC-TV's New York City affiliate.

Grossman founded four businesses: Cruises of Distinction, Office Organix, MyGreenMind.com and the EBook Bakery.

He taught English and Journalism at Oakland Community College and holds B.A. and M.A. degrees from Michigan State University. Currently, Grossman runs the EBook Bakery, a company helping other authors self-publish paperbacks, EBooks and audiobooks.

Born in Muskegon, Michigan, Grossman and his wife currently reside in Rhode Island.